T0352997

The Nicest
Girl

Have you ever wondered how books are made?

UCLan Publishing is an award winning independent publisher specialising in Children's and Young Adult books. Based at The University of Central Lancashire, this Preston-based publisher teaches MA Publishing students how to become industry professionals using the content and resources from its business; students are included at every stage of the publishing process and credited for the work that they contribute.

The business doesn't just help publishing students though. UCLan Publishing has supported the employability and real-life work skills for the University's Illustration, Acting, Translation, Animation, Photography, Film & TV students and many more. This is the beauty of books and stories; they fuel many other creative industries! The MA Publishing students are able to get involved from day one with the business and they acquire a behind the scenes experience of what it is like to work for a such a reputable independent.

The MA course was awarded a Times Higher Award (2018) for Innovation in the Arts and the business, UCLan Publishing, was awarded Best Newcomer at the Independent Publishing Guild (2019) for the ethos of teaching publishing using a commercial publishing house. As the business continues to grow, so too does the student experience upon entering this dynamic Masters course.

www.uclanpublishing.com
www.uclanpublishing.com/courses/
uclanpublishing@uclan.ac.uk

SOPHIE JO

The Nicest Girl

uclanpublishing

Too nice. Too nice. Too nice. Too nice. Too nice.
Too nice. Too nice. Too nice. Too nice. Too nice.
Too nice. Too nice. Too nice. Too nice. Too nice.
Too nice. Too nice. Too nice. Too nice. Too nice.
Too nice. Too nice. Too nice. Too nice. Too nice.
Too nice. Too nice. Too nice. Too nice. Too nice.
Too nice. Too nice. Too nice. Too nice. Too nice.
Too nice. Too nice. Too nice. Too nice. Too nice.
Too nice. Too nice. Too nice. Too nice. Too nice.
Too nice. Too nice. Too nice. Too nice. Too nice.
Too nice. Too nice. Too nice. Too nice. Too nice.
Too nice. Too nice. Too nice. Too nice. Too nice.
Too nice. Too nice. Too nice. Too nice. Too nice.
Too nice. Too nice. Too nice. Too nice. Too nice.
Too nice. Too nice. Too nice. Too nice. Too nice.
Too nice. Too nice. Too nice. Too nice. Too nice.
Too nice. Too nice. Too nice. Too nice. Too nice.
Too nice. Too nice. Too nice. Too nice. Too nice.
Too nice. Too nice. Too nice. Too nice. Too nice.
Too nice. Too nice. Too nice. Too nice. Too nice.
Too nice. Too nice. Too nice. Too nice. Too nice.
Too nice. Too nice. Too nice. Too nice. Too nice.
Too nice. Too nice. Too nice. Too nice. Too nice.
Too nice. Too nice. Too nice. Too nice. Too nice.
Too nice. Too nice. Too nice. Too nice. Too nice.

The Nicest Girl is a uclanpublishing book

First published in Great Britain in 2022 by
uclanpublishing
University of Central Lancashire
Preston, PR1 2HE, UK

978-1-912979-96-7

1 3 5 7 9 10 8 6 4 2

Set in 10.5/17pt Kingfisher by Becky Chilcott.

A CIP catalogue record for this book is available from the British Library.

Printed and bound in Great Britain by Clays Ltd, Elcograf S.p.A.

For anyone who's ever had trouble saying no

One

I love you, but sometimes I need a break.

That is what I would say to Marla if I was a different sort of person.

> **Marla 23:07**
> anna

> **Marla 23:07**
> babe it's all gone wrong again

> **Marla 23:07**
> can i talk to you??

Sometimes, when I'm trying to sleep at night, I picture that person in my head. I don't have a name for her, but I can see her, and she doesn't look like me.

She doesn't *act* like me, either. She's loud. Direct. Someone who doesn't have any kind of filter, but never in a way that gets her into trouble. People think she's great.

I know for certain that if three predictably anxious messages from her best friend arrived just as she was going to bed, she'd ignore them. She'd say, *I need to sleep, so let's talk tomorrow, OK?*

Marla 23:08
are you still up??? my heart is breaking and i need u

This girl commands attention. In a social situation, if she speaks at the same time as another person, you'll always choose her to listen to. No one ever talks about that, but we all know it happens. It's like the decision is made instantly, in a part of your brain that doesn't even register it.

Everybody loves how authentic she is – how she never tries to be something else, or someone else. They all say that she's outspoken. Transparent. Stuff like that.

No one, not a single soul in this world, would ever describe her as *nice.*

Anna 23:11
oh marls

Anna 23:12
what's happened?

Marla 23:16

well i asked him who becky is and apparently she's some
girl he met on a residential week away in year 10 and
they aren't even really in touch any more but i've just got
a feeling about it. said to him LOOK CARL if you would
prefer to date a girl from your childhood school trip then
just tell me!!! and he was like ugh not this again it needs
to stop blah blah. and then i went all weird and he sighed
really loud and said marla i'm tired maybe you should just
go so i DID and i think i have ruined it, for real this time

Marla 23:16

thoughts???

I take a deep breath in, then out, in, then out. Then I switch
the bedside lamp back on, prepared for its second shift of the
evening. *Becky*.

Last term, it was Naina from Carl's chemistry class. Over the
summer it was Chloe, the family friend he has known since he
was six. And now, right on cue, attention has shifted over to
Becky, who popped up on Carl's phone a few hours ago and
sent Marla down a whole new trail of worry.

It exhausts me when I think about all this too hard, because
I can't imagine living in a world where you believe everybody
cares about your boyfriend as much as you do. I like Carl
a lot, but I'm not convinced of his universal appeal. I'm not

convinced of anyone's universal appeal, really. Surely even the most beautiful person in the world wouldn't do it for everybody. The funniest person wouldn't be funny to all of us. No matter what happened, there would still be a few people on earth who would say, *no, thank you, not for me.*

But Marla *is* convinced, and also very vigilant.

We walk to sixth form together on weekdays, and when she shows up at my house each morning I'll ask her, *is everything OK now?* Sometimes she'll have forgotten all about it, and instead will talk about the length of her eyelashes or some gloomy-sounding film she wants me to promise I'll watch. But most of the time, she will sigh with her chest before she starts to recount the update. *Where to begin, AC. Where to begin.*

She calls me AC because we realised that Anna is a truly unshortenable name. Marla becomes Marls, usually, which is kind of unofficial-sounding but works quite well. It's a nice word to say. But Anna can't really become anything, except maybe Ann, which is a whole other name that isn't my own and feels nothing like me. So, Anna Campbell is now AC. I don't like it much, and I've told her: Anna is fine.

Anna is always fine.

Anna 23:18

i know it's hard but he really loves you!! you've worried about this stuff before and it's never been worth it. you're carl and marla.

CARLA remember?? who else could he have that with ♥

Marla 23:19
yeah but this time it's different. my stomach hurts anna
i really think he might be done

Marla 23:19
carl and becky. BARL! CECKY!!!!

Anna 23:20
cecky schmecky. he won't be done!

Marla 23:21
great news i've found her tiktok and she is basically
a hotter version of me

Anna 23:21
☹ she isn't! please exit the app as a matter
of urgency

Anna 23:27
are you still looking??

Marla 23:28
still looking still trying not to cry over becky's
stupid perfect face!!!

Marla 23:28

he hasn't even messaged to see if i'm OK. he doesn't even care. i left his house at half 10 and he probably fell asleep in 30 seconds dreaming about his new life as one half of cecky

Anna 23:29

'one half of cecky' sounds like they have started a terrible band together. i for one will not be listening to cecky

Marla 23:34

lmao. cecky's first album will be called GOODBYE MARLA WE ARE IN LOVE

Anna 23:36

no, they will release one single called MARLA WAS WRONG – WE AREN'T A THING!! SIMPLY OLD ACQUAINTANCES WHO OCCASIONALLY WISH EACH OTHER GLAD TIDINGS VIA IMESSAGE

Marla 23:45

yes yes alright i take the point

Anna 23:47

good ☺ will you be able to sleep?

Marla 00:01

maybe baby. i'll try. see you tomorrow at 8 at yours??

love you love you

Anna 00:03

perfect. i love you too ♥

Tomorrow at eight at mine.

First day of Year 13.

It's past midnight now. Tomorrow is today. *Perfect.*

I lie in the dark again for a while, stubbornly waiting for sleep. My brain is somehow buzzier than it was an hour ago, as if now it knows Wednesday is here it no longer sees the point in going to bed at all. As if now it knows Marla is struggling, it feels obligated to stay on high alert. This happens a lot.

There's a small rectangle of light on my ceiling, poking its way in from the streetlamps outside. I sigh – a loud, unnecessary sigh I would never perform in front of another person – and heave myself out of bed, ready to banish the offending shape. Before I rearrange the curtains, I pull them back and gaze out of the window, standing on tiptoes to look up and down the road. It's completely still out there. There are no lights on in any of the houses I can see and the discovery makes me feel strange, as though the world is suddenly empty and all of the people are gone.

Back in bed, I pick up my phone again and start to scroll

through the same stuff as always. *Don't worry*, it says, a portal to a land that isn't dark and silent. *Things are happening. We are alive. Everyone is right here.* The thought calms me. I laugh quietly at something and forward it to Marla, captioning underneath with: me and u. She doesn't reply.

12:37 a.m.

1:10 a.m.

A car races past and the people inside it must be tired, same as I am. Where do they need to get to? Why is anybody still awake? I pull the duvet tight around me like a hood and try my hardest to think of nothing. If I was a different sort of person, I'd have been asleep two hours ago.

Two

My yawns are big and I don't fancy cereal and my dad raises his brow when I tell him I slept fine. He glances at me in a semi-concerned sort of way as he answers his phone with the usual 'Paul Campbell?' and starts to make notes on a scrap of paper next to the salt and pepper pots. I assess my eyebags in the hallway mirror. They could be worse.

When Marla rings the doorbell in her usual fashion – three confident prods, one immediately after the other – I perk up a little. She seems cheerful for someone who spent their weekend panicking over an impending break-up, hugging me like she doesn't have any recollection of our bedtime discussion, but I know her well enough to guess this is for my dad's benefit.

'Helloooooo, Paul!' she calls, peering around the doorframe. Her short black bob dangles down on one side as she grins. My dad glances up from the dining table, distracted, and waves gently in Marla's direction as he continues his conversation.

She retracts her head, wiggling on the spot like a restless child while I sit on the bottom stair to put my shoes on. When I mouth goodbye to my dad, he offers me a banana from the fruit bowl next to him – first wordlessly, then with slightly more vigour when I shake my head. I take the banana and put it in my pocket.

I always feel nervy on the first day of term, like everything could have changed and I might be the only person not to know it. Like there's a chance everyone else had some sort of meeting over the summer that I wasn't told about, where they all decided things without me. I ask Marla if Year 13 is supposed to feel that way, or if the nervy feeling is supposed to have gone by now.

'It's definitely supposed to have gone,' says Marla, deadpan. 'But the meeting was great. I told them not to invite you.'

I snort and she wrinkles her nose at me as she bites a nail, her eyes playful. She's wearing her usual ancient leather jacket on top of a floaty black dress with sunflowers tiled across it, and there are matching yellow studs attached proudly to her ears. She looks like a children's TV presenter, in the best way.

'You're the worst,' I say. 'Don't you ever get first-day anxiety?'

Marla shakes her head. 'No. It's the same mediocre people in the same mediocre place. What would anyone need to be anxious about?'

I used to have this recurring nightmare, almost every time I went on holiday as a kid, that all of my friends would forget about me. And that I would come back – suntanned and freckled, with one of those colourful braids in my long hair that my mum would need to cut out with scissors before school started – and everyone would say, *we're just not bothered about Anna now. Actually, we got on better without her. We didn't even notice she was gone.* My first day nerves feel more or less like that, except I'm not seven any more.

'I don't know.' It isn't the sort of thing I can explain out loud. I want to talk about something else, something that'll take my mind off the day ahead of us. 'Did Carl message you this morning?'

Marla nods morosely, then pauses. I hug my cardigan around me while I wait for her to elaborate, rubbing my hands along my upper arms as we walk. I'm one of those people who is always cold. Socks in bed, even in summer. I think it's bad circulation.

'Yeah. He said he was sorry we argued and that I need to stop bringing up Becky and that he is allowed to have friends and acquaintances who are girls just like I have friends and acquaintances who are boys.'

Her voice sounds stony and sarcastic, like she's being forced to write lines with her mouth, but she still looks at me questioningly after she's finished speaking – big eyes, sad face – wanting me to confirm if Carl's perspective is worthy of an apology from her end.

'Marls, I—'

She interrupts. 'He doesn't understand that I have these two different halves to my brain, OK? I tried to explain to him – like, there's the good half, and it comes out sometimes, and it'll tell me to calm down and remember all the happy stuff. But when the other half kicks in, I *cannot* get it to stop. It won't let me sleep and I don't get hungry and I just sit there for hours thinking of a million different shitty scenarios because I *know* he'll find somebody better and I *know* he'll break up with me.'

The thing about Marla is that she listens but instantly forgets. I know it, so I know how this will go. We'll talk through everything – me offering recycled reassurance, diluted truths, whatever else – and she'll nod at the end of it, and she'll say, *you're right. He loves me. I need to remember that.* And I'll say something encouraging, like, *you're the best! You should* always *remember that!* But she won't. It wipes me out, same as the bedtime messages. I love Marla so much that sometimes I feel an ache in my stomach when I think about her, like nostalgia and excitement combined. I just wish she'd take a day off from worrying every once in a while. Maybe then I could, too.

It's started to drizzle so I open my umbrella, holding it up awkwardly over both of us in a way that feels charitable but pointless at the same time. I'm so much taller than Marla that this act never seems to be of much benefit to her, and she *ughs* when the rain gets heavier, moving in towards me for protection. I try to shrink while I pull the umbrella down as close to my head as it'll go. Marla picks at a nail on her right hand. The skin around it has started to bleed and she inspects it for a second before holding the finger to her mouth to suck, like a sad vampire. I want to find her a plaster. I want to ask, *if your boyfriend is so wonderful, why are you always convinced he's going to leave you?*

She catches me looking and somehow reads my mind. 'I know you don't get it. But it's like . . . it's like, do you remember when my nana was ill? And everyone kept saying, "oh, it's so good she caught it early. You should always look out for the signs and catch it before it gets too bad"?' I nod. 'Well, it feels a bit like that. Maybe if I watch out for it, I can catch it early. And then it won't get too bad.'

Marla and I met on the first day of Year 7. She was sitting on my table in Miss Lee's class, and we were each given a sticky label and a felt-tip pen and told to write our name with an alliterative word in front of it. *So* I *would be Happy Harriet,* said the girl next to us, presenting Marla with a syrupy smile she didn't look keen to return. *And Anna would be Abnormal Anna,* grunted a boy further down, smirking at the kid opposite him before making eye contact to clarify that he didn't like me. *Oh, big words from Nauseating Nathan!* Marla snapped, quick as lightning. Nathan said, *yeah, well,* and didn't speak again for the rest of the lesson. He was expelled in Year 10 and we never found out why, but Marla has a wide range of theories.

We've always been different, but never in a way that wouldn't work. Sometimes different is better, like when she forced me to try a vegan burger for the first time and I enjoyed it more than the beef version and she said, *told you, didn't I.* Or when she comes out with a Marla-sharp commentary on someone I also think is ridiculous but would never outwardly condemn, and it makes me laugh so hard I feel sick. I know us well enough now, and I am a watercolour – pale and forgettable. Easy enough to change or smudge. Just . . . *nice.* Marla is the bright oil painting next to me – bold and difficult. She wants you to look at her. She will take weeks to dry.

Marla glances up from the floor and I take one of her shaky arms as we approach the Broadacre High entrance, linking mine through hers like she's a frail old lady. It takes us a few seconds to sync our steps and stop bumping sides, and she smiles when I knock into her hip deliberately to try and bring the mood back up. She's still waiting for me to say something. Anything at all.

'I get it, Marls,' I offer, finally. We huddle tight under the umbrella and I mentally sift through a drawer of motivational quotes, throwing irrelevant ones to the side and highlighting lines of others ready to use, just like I've done every other day for the last few months. 'I do. But I guess you just need to . . . listen to the sensible half of your brain. Try to ignore the bad bit. Carl likes *you.* Every girl you've worried about has been a false alarm, and even if they were trying to get his attention, I don't think he'd care.'

'You don't *think* he'd care. Carl doesn't *think* he'd find some other girl at his sixth form. Where are the people who *know*?'

Her eyes flash, panicked, as the noise from the Broadacre grounds grows louder.

'Marla! Anna! *Finally.*' Aleks waves from a bench. She and Natalie have spotted us, and the next few moments are all hugs and laughter, summer in-jokes, first-day compliments. Marla tries to smile.

The good half of her brain is hard to reach this morning, and I hate that I've said anything to make this worse. I reach for her hand, find it, squeeze it tight. *I'm sorry. I've got you.* She looks up at me, listless, and squeezes back.

I was trying to make it better. I'm always trying to make it better.

Three

The sixth form welcome session drags, as expected. *Great to be back / final year / appropriate clothing / believe and you will achieve.* I try to stifle my yawns but Aleks embraces hers, rolling her eyes so far back into her head I can only see white. We grin at each other. She's dyed her hair Little Mermaid red over the summer – banned at Broadacre – and every teacher that spots her shoots a *see me afterwards* look in our direction. Natalie is dressed in her sports kit already, poised to dash away for football or hockey or something else energetic. The familiarity of it makes my shoulders relax.

As we file out of the hall, a man's voice calls my name. I stop and turn back to assess where it's coming from, and three Year 10 girls give me a dirty look for blocking their path. I tell them I'm sorry – the muttered, automatic kind of sorry – and move to the side to stand against a sports day display wall while I wait for the owner of the voice to reach me.

Mr Bains, our head of sixth form. He's got someone next to him – a tall, skinny boy with sandy hair and a backpack that looks like it could have been purchased this morning. The boy gives me a brief half-a-mouth smile before becoming very interested in the sports day display. He's holding a small bottle of half-drunk orange juice and I can see him picking at the label with one thumb, the same way Marla pokes at the skin next to her fingernails. Although he looks about my age and has a Broadacre lanyard around his neck, I've never seen him before in my life.

'This is *Ryan*, Anna,' Mr Bains says. He's going to great pains to enunciate perfectly, as though backpack boy – *Ryan* – is five years old or doesn't speak good English. 'His family's just moved to Broadacre, so Ryan'll be spending Year 13 with us.'

No wonder the boy seems dazed. He nods without looking at me, gripping one backpack strap tightly with his free hand. The knuckles are ghost-white.

'Anna, you showed Natalie Tam around the school way back when she started here for Year 9, didn't you?' Mr Bains continues, and I nod, dread sprinting up the sides of my stomach as I realise where this is going. 'Well, I'd like you to do the same for Ryan, please. A *Broadacre Buddy*, if you will.'

I laugh out of politeness, like always, but Ryan doesn't. Mr Bains's smile stays fixed. 'Ryan'll be joining your form, so for this first term you'll be the one to look out for him. Show him the ropes, bring him up to speed.' His eyes are solid expectation.

'How does that sound?'

It doesn't sound good.

At some point – around Year 8, I think, but possibly before – I managed to position myself as some sort of go-to girl within the Broadacre community. I feel like it started when Mrs Wilson needed people to decorate the form room for Christmas and nobody put their hand up to volunteer. She looked so sad as the Santa pin badge on her shirt flashed to a blank-faced class. *Guess I'll be putting the tree up on my own, then, 8B.* So I told her I'd help, which I did, and then I helped again when she needed to take the decorations down in January, even though that task is never not depressing. After that, Anna Campbell had somehow become the person who would always say yes. That's why I ended up showing Natalie around the school in Year 9, even though I was one of the shyer girls in our class back then and the thought of spending week upon week with the new kid was enough to make me feel faintly ill with nerves. Natalie smiled with her entire face, cheerfully vulnerable, already sunshine in a room, but it didn't help. It never really occurred to me that I wasn't the only person for the job – that I could say, *no, thanks. I think I'll sit this one out.*

I have organised bake sales. Helped with homework. Filled in as wing defence for people who've bailed on the day of the netball tournament. Sometimes I want to do it. Other times I'm not so sure. Occasionally I will attempt a 'no', but a 'no' never comes out properly – it ends up as something wordy and apologetic, always punctuated by far too many 'um's and 'sorry's. Marla calls it the Campbell Ramble. She thinks it's funny. To Marla, saying no can be instant and natural – just part of her, like blinks or hiccups. I am clumsier than that. I wrestle with my gut while I weigh it all up, considering everyone and everything, like sick you're trying to keep down while you work out where the nearest bathroom is.

This makes me sound like a pretend person, or a liar. I'm not a liar. I just struggle with the truth sometimes.

In Year 11, we were temporarily friends with this popular girl called Wynn, who seemed to be everywhere for a few months before slowly migrating over to another friendship group and doing the same thing with them. Wynn never seemed to have money for lunch, despite living in one of the massive, detached houses right next to school, and most days she would ask if I could buy food for her. I always did, even though I didn't like Wynn a huge amount, and she would always say, *great! I promise I'll get sorted for next week*, but she never did.

One weekend, two days before our mock GCSEs, when everything was starting to build up and look terrifying, I said to Marla, 'Am I a doormat?' She looked up from drawing on her eyeliner and said, 'Possibly, babe. I wouldn't worry about it.'

I did worry about it. I worried about it a lot, because I could understand Wynn needing to ask for money once or twice, but not as often as she did. My mum kept commenting on how much food I was getting through at school. I felt guilty. I would act out arguments in the shower, imagining showdown situations where I told Wynn 'no', where I questioned the whole thing, but I never brought them outside of the bathroom. In reality, I was afraid that rejecting her request would make people turn against me. That I would snap eventually, get too angry or speak too harshly, and they would say, *wow, Anna is so selfish. She wouldn't even help Wynn when she needed it. What kind of a friend is that?* A few days later, I asked Aleks if *she* thought I was a doormat with Wynn. She looked kind of sad for a moment and said, 'Well, look at it this way – she hasn't asked anyone else to buy stuff for her.'

The term irks me, even now, because an actual doormat isn't a bad thing. It's supposed to be the sign of a welcome – Marla's house has a colourful one in the shape of a rainbow, and everybody comments on how much they like it.

I wish things had changed since Wynn. But they haven't, and I know that they won't, so I smile at Mr Bains and I tell him, 'yes.'

I tell him, 'of course.'

I tell him, 'no problem at all.'

Four

By midway through the day everything feels normal again, as though summer was a film we watched weeks ago and have now forgotten about. Ryan has been instructed to join me for food, and he flounders by our usual cafeteria table for a moment while I sit, gesturing for him to do the same. He chooses a corner seat opposite me – Marla's favourite – and sets up camp there, his back to the wall and his eyes round and blinking.

Little pockets of pupils are filling up the room, waving at familiar faces for the first time in six weeks and shouting over the hum of voices. A few people stare in our direction, trying to work out who the new kid is and why he's here. Ryan clocks them and runs a hand through his hair self-consciously. Broadacre's big, but it's not *that* big. He can't just blend in.

'Have you got lunch with you?' I ask, a surface-level attempt to take his mind off the crowds.

'Yeah, yeah. In my bag. Thanks.' He's moved his attention

to the orange juice bottle in his hand, taking his time to fake-study the label so he doesn't have to make unnecessary eye contact. Or I think that's why, anyway. I'm usually pretty good at working this stuff out.

'*Here* she is. Hey, Anna, what do y—' Natalie's words ring out above the noise, faltering the moment she spots the brand-new boy sitting opposite me. I see her prod Marla, who glares before she understands and immediately thuds down next to me, visibly irritated by the unintentional usurping of her seat.

Natalie beams in Ryan's direction, unfazed. 'Oh! *Hi*.'

Ryan looks up from his orange juice, the tops of his cheeks pinkening. 'All right?'

She nods earnestly as she wanders to the other side of the table to claim a spare seat next to him. He returns the gesture, a sad sort of mirror.

'This is Ryan,' I say quickly. 'He just started today.' It feels uncomfortable to launch into a Broadacre Buddies explanation – too much like an excuse – so I make a split-second decision to tell them about it later, when they can ask questions, when Ryan's not around to feel embarrassed. 'Ryan, these are my friends – Marla and Natalie. Nats, where's Aleks?'

'Emergency climate-change meeting,' says Natalie, her gaze still on Ryan. 'Plastic-themed. Aw, first *day*. I remember that feeling.'

Ryan relaxes slightly. 'You're new, too?'

'*Was*. Not any more. I started in Year 9, though, which I

would not recommend to anybody ever. Where did you live before? I like your accent.'

'Woolton,' Ryan says, eyes on the juice bottle again. 'Liverpool.' Natalie takes the opportunity to mouth *cute!* in my direction, and I smile, grateful for her enthusiasm.

Marla's been chewing a sandwich with her mouth open, staring at Ryan with suspicion from our side of the table. She swallows and wipes her bottom lip with the back of a hand, but says nothing. She can be like this sometimes, like strangers have arrived solely to bother her.

I try to balance it out, same as always. 'How's your morning been, Ryan? Bearable? Terrible?'

He shrugs lightly. 'OK, I guess. Miss James seems pretty nice. Mr Bains is . . . kind of exhausting. Is he always like that?'

Natalie lets out a sharp squawk of laughter. 'I mean . . . he's a lovely man, but yes. Incredibly wholesome all round. It makes you feel *heinous* for ever having had a bad thought about anyone.'

She grins in his direction and Ryan echoes it shakily, willing but nervous. He takes a final safety-swig of orange juice before returning the bottle to his open backpack.

Natalie stares at the bag's innards. 'What are you reading?'

Ryan stiffens. 'What?'

'The book in your bag. What is it?'

'Oh! It's . . . it's Bukowski.' I expect him to show us this Bukowski, whatever it is, but he seems reluctant, zipping the backpack up again so its contents are hidden from view. 'Do you know him?'

Natalie shakes her head. 'Not really. Is he depressing?'

Ryan pauses for a second, considering the question. 'Not to me.'

'I'll do a book swap with you sometime, then. None of these people *read*.' She raises her voice playfully as she points a finger in mine and Marla's direction, and I cover my face with my hands in mock embarrassment.

As the conversation lulls, Marla glances up from her phone, interested at last. Ryan returns the glance gingerly.

'Why are you here . . . *now*? Like, why move schools in Year 13? I can't think of anything worse,' she says, frowning. She seems like she's enquiring because she's genuinely confused – and she's always been braver with this type of thing than I have – but in typical Marla style, it comes out more violently than she hears it.

Ryan immediately sits upright on his stool, piercing the comfortable energy that had started to settle around us. 'Just stuff with my family,' he mumbles, after a long-enough silence. Even Marla can tell this is not a topic he wants anyone to push. She backs off and returns to her phone, tapping her thumbs on the screen with more effort than usual while Ryan crumples back down to his original position.

It already feels like my job to diffuse the tension – to scramble around for less combative conversation, even though I only met this boy three hours ago and know next to nothing about him. Marla sniffs, shows Natalie something on her phone, pretends Ryan isn't here, and Mr Bains nods knowingly in my direction as he walks past our table with a boxed salad.

Just stuff with my family. I don't know what that would mean.

I see Ryan lingering by the school gates at the end of the day, his phone in one hand and a new orange juice in the other. *That's three bottles he brought with him, minimum*, I think, *so this is definitely a thing.* For a second, I wonder if I could sneak past undetected. Double back, ask Marla to meet me at the other entrance, shake him off until tomorrow and hope he bonds with some other group in the meantime so this entire Broadacre Buddies set-up can be forgotten forever.

But as I hesitate, he spots me. 'All right, Anna?' Too late. I quicken my pace slightly to get to him. 'Just waiting on my mum to pick me up. She said she'd text when she got here,' he says, waving his phone as proof.

I don't really know how to respond to this and I'm nervous to ask more about his family after the uncomfortable reaction to Marla's lunchtime question, so I smile and pretend to survey the crowds like he's doing. After a second, he turns towards me. 'Thanks for the help today. It's nice, to have someone around.'

'Oh! No, it's fine,' I say, surprised by his gratitude. 'It must have been a strange day for you.'

There's a prolonged pause while I wait for Ryan to respond, to confirm that this *has* been a strange day for him. He doesn't.

'So . . . what kind of stuff do you like doing?' I ask, wanting to vanquish the silence. The question feels banal in my mouth again, an effort, a tame kind of offering.

Ryan looks at me blankly. 'Well, I sailed in Liverpool.'

'Sailing!' I say, as if I know lots about it. 'That sounds fun.' It doesn't sound fun at all, but I'm not sure what else would be appropriate to fill the gap here. Ryan looks pleased and I feel fraudulent. I wish Natalie was here to help this flow.

'It is. It *was*.' There's another silence, then a car down the road beeps its horn and Ryan gives it a short thumbs-up. As he takes his backpack from the floor and swings it on to one shoulder, he turns to me with slightly more urgency than before. 'Anna, can I maybe have your number? It's fine if not, obviously. I just thought . . . '

Poor Ryan. He trails off, like I can probably guess what he thought. I can guess he needs a friend, and I feel guilty for not wanting it to be me. It isn't that I don't like him – he seems kind among his nervousness, his face flushed pink again as he awkwardly pokes at a leaf with one shoe. But I know this for certain: we wouldn't have flowed towards each other naturally. We wouldn't have had this conversation without first being pushed.

The car beeps again and Ryan coughs, like he needs a decision, fast. I picture packing up my life – shoving everything into boxes and then unloading it all in a brand-new place, already knowing it wouldn't come out the same – and for the third or fourth time today I think, *I would not want to be you.*

'Of course you can,' I say, softening. 'Here, let me put it in your phone.'

I've made tomato pasta for when Dad finishes work, which can be any time between 5 and 7 p.m. depending on the kind of things he needs to get done. He works from home, usually at the big dining table in the living room, which I have told him is a terrible idea for ergonomic reasons. We have an evening routine now, rarely altered because we're both used to it and my dad doesn't really like change. Although, I realise, he *did* used to be the designated Campbell family chef. Slowly, it's somehow become my role.

'Thanks, love,' he says, yawning as he closes down the laptop. 'Sorry I wasn't with it earlier – it's been insane. How was day one?'

How *was* day one? I try to pick something vaguely exciting to report on and opt for Ryan, waiting for a response or any words of advice while my dad disappears into the hallway to collect something that's just clattered through the letterbox.

The kitchen windows have steamed up with condensation, so I crack one open and spoon pasta on to plates. He returns with a crumpled Farmfoods flyer, temporarily interested in something on the front before he tosses it on to the sofa.

'We'll take the recycling out tomorrow.' When my dad says 'we', he usually means 'Anna'.

I nod, searching for cutlery.

Things in the Campbell household are what Marla calls 'bland'. You know how there are those families that are loud and full and welcoming? They usually have a pet, and a liberal open-door policy, and sometimes a ping-pong table. And when you go into those houses, you feel instantly relaxed, like you could take a look in the fridge without asking or stop on the sofa for a few days and it'd all be fine. They'd just run with it, because that's what they're like. *Join us for dinner! Make yourself at home.* My family isn't like that. I think bland probably is the right word for it, though that stings a little. Things aren't really bad or good, happy or sad, stop or go. They just sort of tick along, like a slow Sunday where you forget to get dressed until midday. My dad is busy with his design work, most of the time, so he's distracted, and I'm busy with sixth form, and Marla, and everything else, so I don't mind. We are polite housemates now.

At the start of summer, Marla came round with Aleks and Natalie. I'd invited them the week before, so I'd spent time planning what we could do, what we would eat, all of that stuff. It isn't a big deal for Marla to be in my house – she's there almost every day – but the thought of *everyone* coming in, all of us, made me feel nervous. Like it was a test. And the entire evening I was on edge – conscious of the lack of impressive snacks in the cupboards; the quiet we kept disturbing, my dad working below us, Aleks' high-powered laugh. When they left, they all said, *thanks, we had a great time,* but I wasn't convinced.

'How was *your* day, Dad?' I ask as we sit down. We do this too many times a week.

He mutters something about Adobe that doesn't make sense to me, before moving his attention to the large plate of pasta. There's a bunch of discarded papers all over the table – stacks of drawings and mock-ups he's made for clients over the last few weeks. *Still nothing wrong with starting off analogue*, he would tell me when I was younger, pointing one finger like a wise old wizard letting me in on an ancient secret. My mum and I would pretend to snore. One time I said, *Anna-logue!*, proud of myself for the wordplay, and for some reason we all thought it was the funniest thing we'd ever heard.

It's odd that you can live with someone but still hold on to a quiet worry that you might run out of things to discuss with them. I am a *good* conversationalist – the best our family has to offer, now – but my dad has never been a talker. He likes to say *hmm* and *yes* and *I see* and *what about this weather, eh*, and that's not because everything else you might deem important isn't in his head, because it is, but it doesn't come out very often. I mean, it must have done with my mum, because you don't marry someone who only says *hmm* and *yes* and *I see* and *what about this weather, eh*. I know that you don't. But my mum kind of balanced him out, I think. She told all the stories and threw all the parties, so he wasn't really required to tell or throw himself. Without her here, there isn't anyone to do any of that now. I've taken on the cleaning, the thinking, the talking. Most of the work, but none of the clout.

My phone flashes for a second:

> **Ryan 18:32**
> Hey Anna its Ryan. Thanks again for showing me round.

> **Anna 18:34**
> no worries!! see you tomorrow – welcome to join us for
> lunch again ☺

He sends me a thumbs-up, a little smiley with its teeth on show, like it's a given. I guess neither of us have much of a choice.

Five

By the time the weekend rolls around, Marla seems intermittently brighter – a light bulb on the blink. We're in her kitchen eating delivery pizza (pepperoni for me, vegan margherita for her) and discussing the fact that Natalie is rarely seen in the same outfit more than once.

'It's an environmental disgrace, really,' says Marla, swallowing, 'but you've got to admit that she does look very good.' I murmur in agreement and Marla grins with her tongue resting between her teeth. She's wearing red dungarees and a striped, long-sleeved tee; with one leg up on the breakfast stool she's almost cartoonish.

The kitchen door clicks open as Marla's mum, Joelle, wafts in for the second time this evening. She's biting down on a pencil, eyes busy, clearly looking for something, and it makes Marla scowl. 'God, what do you *need*?'

Joelle stops rooting through a drawer near the microwave

and pulls an identical face. She looks exactly how I think Marla will in twenty-five years – it's like Mr Mackinlay was never involved at all. I can hear him upstairs, whistling some 90s song I can't remember the name of.

'Has anybody seen that booklet thing that came through the door?' Joelle asks. 'The yellow one? It had a load of odd-job stuff in it and a few ads for local babysitters.'

I'm not sure who she means by *anybody* but I still shake my head earnestly, pretending I'm a member of the family. Joelle thanks me in an absent-minded sort of way, turning her attention to a paper-stuffed box file near the kettle. There's a tiny trickle of water on its way down the outside of my glass and I catch it with one finger, stroking at the rest of the condensation afterwards until it's all disappeared. Marla, flicking a rogue bit of tomato from one side of her plate to another, doesn't say anything. I can tell she wants Joelle to continue the search elsewhere.

'What did you need it for?' I offer after a few seconds, keen to fill the gap. Marla can sit with an awkward silence much better than I can.

'Maybe your dad's seen it,' Joelle murmurs distractedly, biting her lip and looking at Marla. Then she remembers my question. 'Oh! Babysitters, really, Anna. I've got a friend who needs someone to take care of her four year old on a Tuesday evening and she's struggling to find a sitter. Oh, *Marls*, you wouldn't do it, would you, darling?'

I know Marla will say no, because Tuesday is Carl night. They watch films and eat Mexican food together. Sometimes Carl makes other Tuesday plans and offers Marla a different weekday option. This has never gone down well.

Marla scoffs. 'No. You know I don't want kids.' She gets down from the stool, flouncing to the sink to refill her water cup. One of her socks has a hole in the heel.

'I'm not asking you to *have* one. I'm asking you to *look after* one. For a few hours. Once a week,' says Joelle slowly, like she's bored.

'It's Carl night, anyway.'

'Couldn't you move Carl night?'

'I couldn't, actually.'

Marla sits back down, taking a loud sip of her drink as she does so, and Joelle makes a noise that's a half-tut, half-sigh. 'I had a look online but you have to sign up to this whole agency website and it all seems like a bit of a hassle. The booklet was right *here* this morning – that's the only reason I mentioned it to Malini. She's got enough on her plate without me going back to her empty-handed.'

She draws herself back up from hunching over the counter, exasperated, then pauses for a second before her expression changes. 'Anna, what about you?'

Sometimes I feel like I only agree to things because I'm scared that *not* agreeing would make the other person sad. Like when Natalie asked me to join the Broadacre Book Club with her and I told her I would, even though I couldn't remember the last time I'd read anything for fun, because romance novels are one of Natalie's favourite things and turning it down felt too personal, like I would have been spitting on her interests. Or when my dad was convinced it would be fun for us to watch *Breaking Bad* together and I didn't want to hurt his feelings, so he bought an old box set from eBay and I sat through all five seasons with him, enjoying none.

What if Joelle and this other woman – this Malini – don't find anyone else? What if I'm their last option? Joelle doesn't want to go back empty-handed, and it's only one night a week. That's something I could do.

Another voice chimes in, indignant. *You're busy! A million people have already told you how hectic this year is going to be. Then there's the Art Society, and Book Club, and Marla, and your other friends, and everything at home. Joelle's problem is not your problem. Just tell them you don't want to. Say it.*

I don't say it. I make an indecisive *um* sound, like someone who's ready to be told what to do again.

Joelle jumps in, taking her chance. 'Malini's desperate for the help, and it might only be for this term, too – it depends how she gets on. What do you think?'

'*Anna* doesn't have Carl night,' says Marla, with a mouthful of crust.

I shoot her a look and try to think fast. 'I don't know . . . I haven't done anything like that in ages, Joelle. It just doesn't feel like the best idea. Don't you think she'd be better off with somebody a bit more experienced?' I pause, trying to read Joelle's face. She still looks as hopeful as she did thirty seconds ago.

The Campbell Ramble is in action. This is my *no*. This is my *ask someone else; maybe I have a Carl night-equivalent you know nothing about*. I want so badly for Joelle to pick up on it, to read the embarrassed undertone and neatly analyse my awkward body language and say, *yes, of course, no worries*, like I would for her. But she doesn't. Instead of deterring her, I've made her think I'm simply doubting my child-entertainment abilities.

'Nonsense,' she smiles, her eyes wide and appreciative. 'I'll text Malini now. You're doing me a *huge* favour, Anna.'

Marla pushes me the last slice of pepperoni and I feel part of my insides crumble away.

Malini 22:32

Hi Anna, Malini here. Joelle says you'd be happy to babysit for Charlie on Tuesdays? Lifesaver! Is next Tuesday OK, the 15th?

Anna 22:44

hi malini! yes, no worries, i can do the 15th! what time works for you?

Have some exclamation marks, Malini! No worries at all!

Malini 22:46

Perfect! Charlie is 4 – he's quite shy but loves to talk about dogs with anyone and everyone. Could you do 6.30pm? I'll need to leave at 6.45pm normally but this just gives us some extra time to chat and for you to meet Charlie. Have heard wonderful things about you from Joelle!

Anna 23:00

cute! i will also talk about dogs with anyone and everyone, haha. course, where abouts are you?

Malini 23:03

We're 73 Jardine, not far from Joelle and Don. Give me a shout if you have any trouble finding us. Thanks again Anna! X

Six

We talk about Carl every day. About his friends, and his football team, and his birthday, which is the day before Halloween. About what Marla might wear to his party, if he has one, which he definitely will. About his past relationships, and his sisters, and the birthmark on his left arm.

I hear about his schedule: boys' night on Friday.

'And that is why we should have *girls'* night on Friday,' says Marla dreamily, as we queue in the toilets midweek. Her breath smells faintly of onions, which means mine will too, because we ate the same thing for lunch. I pluck a packet of elderly peppermint gum from the caverns of my bag and offer it to her, taking one for myself while she decides. She wiggles on the spot as we chew in unison, a dance she always does when she's bored of waiting. Then she remembers what she said a few seconds ago. 'Oh my god. *So!* Girls' night. Food. Me. You, obviously. We'll ask Nats and Aleks, too.'

She says this like it's a definite, rather than a proposal, and tells me about a new Italian restaurant – 'Niccolo's!' – she wants to visit because she's heard very good things about the garlic bread. I tell her I'm in. I like garlic bread as much as the next person. Aleks and Natalie say the same thing, though Aleks winces at the concept of 'girls' night'. For a second I wonder if Marla is potentially less bothered about spending time with her friends and more determined to distract herself while Carl is busy, but I tell myself I'm probably being cynical. There's never any point in saying that sort of thing out loud.

Marla mentions girls' night so many times on Friday that I'm half-expecting her to pull out matching T-shirts for us all.

'Carl says *they're* going out in town tonight, too,' she says, scrolling through her phone as we squeeze on to a common room sofa. 'So we might even see them.'

I make a semi-interested noise, an *mmm*, and she grins at me, shuffling further up to make room for Natalie. There's space for three if you want to be comfortable, but we normally manage four – there's never enough seating in the common room, so you have to take what you can get. Sometimes I'll perch on the arm of the sofa to make things easier for everyone. Sometimes Marla will, too, but because she thinks it makes her look casual and devil-may-care.

'Is Ryan coming with us later, Anna?' asks Natalie.

Ryan's become part of our group, sort of, if only because he's stuck so closely to Mr Bains's Broadacre Buddies plan. He eats with us. He sits next to us in the weekly form meeting. He's quiet, but still there. I'd expected him to make friends elsewhere – organic, unforced friends – and slope off, the same way Wynn-the-lunch-money-girl did. But he seems loyal to the agreement he's put in place, turning up to sixth form with promises he'll join Natalie's Book Club and questions for Aleks, who's warmed to his interest in her climate activism. Today, though, he's nowhere to be seen.

'I don't think he's come in at all – he didn't show up to design class this morning,' says Aleks. She's wearing fishnet tights with tiny rips in them. I can't tell if the rips have been added through wear and tear or deliberate vandalism, but either looks good. 'I wanted to see if he'd stopped bringing those plastic bottles in; he promised me he was gonna get something reusable for his orange juice habit. We *shook* on it. It's a bit weird to be off so early in the term.'

'Not really,' says Natalie. 'If he's ill, he's ill, isn't he? The common cold can strike anytime.'

'True,' I say. 'Maybe I *should* message him and see if he wants to come tonight? He doesn't have real friends yet, does he? Just us.'

Natalie nods, her silver hoop earrings bouncing as she does, but Marla shakes her head at the exact same time, groaning.

It's amicable stalemate, but I'd put money on the fact that Marla will win this round. She normally does.

'Ugh. Do what you want,' she sighs loftily, 'but this is supposed to be *girls'* night, and I for one am not excited to catch the new kid's chesty cough.'

Aleks and Natalie shrug, already moving on to the next topic among themselves. Marla scrunches her nose up, victorious.

We manage to get one of those four-seaters on the train, a little cube so we can all sit opposite each other. Marla and Natalie hate going backwards but Aleks and I don't care that much, so we take the less coveted seats. It's a slow train, one of the long-suffering local ones that stops everywhere.

Ryan messages me as we step off to walk towards the restaurant.

Ryan 19:07
Hey sorry I wasn't around today

Anna 19:09
hey! you were off sick, right? feeling better now?

Ryan 19:10

No. Am ok, probs back Monday. Long story but my
dad turned up. So it's been a bit mental here.

I read the words again, trying to decipher what they might mean. Where did Ryan's dad turn up to? Was he . . . not supposed to do that? Are Broadacre Buddies expected to check in about things that take place outside of sixth form hours? *Who knows,* I think. *Nobody, because there's only one Broadacre Buddy, and it's me.*

I decide to investigate. It feels like he might want me to.

Anna 19:13

ohh – is that a good thing or a bad thing? sounds kind
of bad??

He's *typing* . . . for a few minutes, stopping and starting. Pausing. Then he goes offline. I check my phone again as we enter Niccolo's, then once more as our food arrives at the table. *Last seen today at 19:17.*

Aleks takes her pizza from the waiter, bright-eyed, and continues telling us about her post-detention showdown with Mr Decker, Broadacre's headteacher.

'I was planning to leave calmly but he got me properly riled so I told him he's a fascist and he said "that is very extreme, Aleksandra" and I said "so are your oppressive hair rules,

Mr Decker". He knows I'm right. Tiwa from Year 11 told me he still hasn't bothered to meet with her, and she's been trying to speak to him about Black hair since about 1987.'

While Aleks is talking, I tune out and take her in. Her red hair has started to fade a little now, turning from the bright ketchup of the summer to more of a grungy, sun-flushed peach. There's pen all over her hands – biro song-lyric tattoos – and she's using them to emphasise what she's saying, banging on the table gently and ignoring the glances of diners at the booths next to us.

My mum always used to like Aleks the best. *That girl tells it like it is,* she would say. It didn't seem to work as well when I tried to tell it like it was. I sounded off-brand – where Aleks was brave and honest, I came across gloomy and negative. Some days it bothered me, but other days it didn't. I would just think, *maybe there are some people in life who are supposed to do the telling, and some other people who are supposed to do the listening.* I still don't know.

The restaurant is that nice kind of busy, the kind where there's a hum of sound and it feels exciting to be there, like you are part of whatever Saturday evening has to offer, but where it's not so packed-in that you feel as if you have to leave very soon to make space for someone else. A waitress comes over with a jug and four glasses, apologising for the delay, and I thank her and pour water for everyone, making sure to place myself last like I was taught. I wonder what would have happened if I'd given myself the first glass. The more I consider it, the more I'm convinced no one would have noticed or minded at all. I really hate that I think about stuff like this.

A baby shrieking at the table next to us brings me back to my body.

'Thanks,' says Aleks, taking a gulp of her water. 'Anna, are you still OK to help with the protest planning? We need to do some flyering soon. Stuff like that.'

I nod, and she blows me a kiss from across the table. Then she mutters, 'Where's the *bathroom* in this place?' and hurries off towards the bar, leaving us a temporary three.

Natalie has scraped her long dark hair up into a ponytail – 'or it'll go in the pasta; it's happened before!' – and when I go to check my phone again she seems to sense something's not quite right. 'What's up?'

'It's Ryan,' I tell her, showing his latest messages to the rest of the table. I wait while they read, guilt gently beginning to bite at me as I realise that this might not be something Ryan had wanted to broadcast beyond our WhatsApp conversation.

Natalie hands the phone back to me, blinking with confusion. 'I don't get it. Why would his dad showing up be a bad thing?'

There's no answer to that question yet – just a bunch of ideas and theories starting to sprout in my mind like tiny, anxious plants. *What do we know about Ryan?* Not a lot. He told me this week that they live at his grandparents' house. That the move was quite rushed. He's mentioned his mum. He doesn't like to talk about it. And now his dad is here. *Was* here? I pull a face.

'No idea. Maybe the dad doesn't have a good relationship with them all? Ryan's never actually mentioned him before. I should probably ask.'

'Look, there is literally *nothing* about this that is our problem,' Marla says, staring at a breadstick she's twirling in one hand.

'What d'you mean?' asks Natalie. She sounds surprised. There's a thin sprig of hair that's escaped from her ponytail and is sticking out sideways, wafting around near her ear. I get an urge to tuck it back in again.

Marla swallows a bite of the breadstick, deliberately taking her time. She once told me that you can never underestimate the value of a theatrical pause. Then she sighs. 'Who *cares*? Are you not bored of Ryan popping up everywhere? He's dull. And he's clearly just using us until he finds something better, anyway.'

'He's all right,' says Natalie. She's frowning now, unmoving in her seat.

'But he's not our *friend*, is he? He's just some boy who started following us around because Anna's too nice to say no.'

Anna's too nice to say no.

Her words are lazy and unrehearsed – verbal eyerolls – and I feel them like a punch to the face. I pick up my water glass, forming a defensive barrier between me and everyone else, and busy myself with sipping and swallowing, sipping and swallowing, replaying Marla's declaration on a loop.

Aleks arrives back to the table and Natalie – queen of diplomacy – sweeps in to change the subject, asking everyone in attendance for their thoughts on Niccolo's dessert options. The conversation veers in a whole other direction, taking Marla along with it, but I stay rooted to the spot.

If I was Aleks in this scenario, I think, I would always punch back. I would put my Coke down on the table, hard, just hard enough that it spilled out the top on to my hand, but I wouldn't get a napkin or lick it off, I would just leave it there and I would say, *what the fuck, Marla?*

Marla would look up, shocked but ready to fight.

I would carry on, outspoken and sure of myself: *I'm not too* anything. *And maybe if you bothered to dedicate any time to someone who isn't Carl, you'd get why I'm helping Ryan.* Then I would stand up and leave, and Aleks and Natalie would follow me because they knew I was right, and Marla would call me later in tears to say she was sorry, so so sorry.

Or I'd get jokey, like Natalie always does. I would think of a response instantly, instead of four hours later, and I would say, *well, it's a shame we can't all be selfish like you!* with just the right amount of sass. A playful hit on the arm. And Marla would laugh – *oh my god, AC!* – while everyone else thought, *wow, Anna handled that well.* And even though Marla had laughed, she would know there was something – just a hint of it – that said she had crossed a line. She wouldn't do it again.

But when you're the nice one – not the assertive one, or the tells-it-like-it-is one, or the funny-comebacks one – there is a filter on everything. It all takes time. Words are analysed and reanalysed, birthed and then banished, considered, before being boxed away. Kneejerk reactions aren't allowed. Those are unexpected and disruptive when they come from you; they throw people, so don't bother. Jokes won't work, either, because there's no time to practise and every attempt comes out forced and unnatural. You won't make anyone laugh. So you sit on it, and you overthink it, and you don't do anything.

These are the rules.

I'm weird for the rest of the evening, flitting between quiet embarrassment and a desperate need to show Marla she's wrong. When the waiter brings our bill over and holds out the card machine, I take it wordlessly. As we get up to leave, a man steps in front of us and I barge past him, brushing his side with my shoulder and willing Marla to see me not caring. It doesn't make me feel better at all.

Seven

Most of my weekend is spent staring at the bedroom wall. There's one particular whirl in the paper that looks like a face and I keep focusing on it, eyes fixed on the features until my vision blurs and the same area doesn't really resemble anything at all. I wonder if any other visitors to my room have ever noticed the face, or if I'm the only person in the world to have found it. I make a mental note to ask, *have you seen the face in the wall next to the light switch?* but I know I'll forget. I feel like there is a lot in life that you experience completely alone and without discussion. Like this face-in-the-wall thing, or when you pull a hair out by mistake and for a second before you discard it you examine the white bit at the end that was once in your scalp, or when you're not sure where a shadow on the ceiling is coming from so you wave your hand around in the sunlight to work out what's making it. There are so many moments that feel as if they just take place in my head.

Marla will probably be out doing something with Carl today: eating Sunday burritos and checking his Twitter Likes when he goes to the bathroom. She will probably ask him if he agrees with what she said about me on Friday night and he will probably say, *oh yeah, yeah, you were spot-on, Marls*, just to keep the peace. She will probably message me later to ask something about the history homework, and when I reply I will probably spend an hour and a half crafting what I hope is an obviously irritated message before deleting the whole thing and backtracking entirely.

I keep trying to draw, to make my mind move elsewhere, but nothing is turning out properly and it's messing up my new sketchbook. I've always liked the idea of keeping a tiny A6 book in my bag and adding to it every day, finishing up with a paper collection of whatever it was I was thinking about at the time. Turtles. Houses. Faces. That was the plan when I bought it. *Practise*, like one of those girls on Instagram with the captions that somehow seem modest and braggy at the same time.

Just a quick lunchtime scribble!

10-minute attempt in Starbucks so pls excuse how rough this is . . .

I rip out the first two pages, discarding a seaside and an unwanted cat. The ears are acceptable but I've ruined the nose, and I don't want that here at the front of all this. I scrunch up both of the sheets and toss them out of the way.

Anna's too nice to say no.

I think it would have been better if this had come as a shock. If I'd been bobbing along, calm and unaware of this character trait, and then had been stunned by Marla's comment to the point of denial, like a sad X-Factor contestant who is sure they can sing. It's harder when someone tells you something that doesn't surprise you a bit – a familiar fault you keep failing to bury. I want her to be wrong, but she isn't, and the tops of my shoulders burn with the hurt of it.

For years, I thought it was good to be nice. What was the alternative? Being mean? Rude? Inconsiderate? In my eyes, *nice* and *kind* came from the same family – similar-looking siblings, or possibly even twins. Both meant that you smiled at people, made them feel welcome. Helped them whenever they needed it, no questions asked. But as I got older and everything became more complicated, I started to realise that *nice* wasn't always like *kind* at all. Sometimes *nice* meant letting Marla choose where we ate and what we did and why we did it. It meant saying something was fine with me, even though it wasn't. Sometimes it meant going on dates with boys I didn't like, because I was scared they might feel bad about themselves if I turned them down. *Kind* was when I meant it. *Nice* was when I didn't mean it but wasn't sure I had the right to say so.

At one point – probably two years ago now – I found a

book on my mum's bedside table called *Nice No More*. The book had a bright red cover and promised it could help me using its tried-and-tested techniques – I flicked through and saw that each chapter provided several examples of made-up women learning to shed their niceness and start again. Like Sara:

Sara regularly goes to visit her friends Lucy and Bev, who live a thirty-minute drive away. The three women have been friends for years, but Sara sometimes feels disappointed that all of the plans they make seem to revolve around Lucy and Bev's preferences. For example, Lucy and Bev never suggest meeting near Sara's house. This means Sara is always the friend making the longer journey to Lucy and Bev's village. They then visit the local pub – Lucy's favourite.

Later on, it talked about how the issue had been resolved:

When they meet again, Sara decides to discuss her concerns with Lucy and Bev. She explains that although she loves spending time with them both, she is no longer happy to be the sole traveller when they meet up. Sara has looked on a map to find several midway restaurants – she shows these to her friends, and the three women agree that this is a great idea for the future. Sara is pleased she has found a compromise.

I was pleased Sara had found a compromise, too. I felt happy for her, mostly because she sounded like me, but then I tried to picture the same scenario taking place in real life and couldn't. It struck me how neat and simple everything seemed in Sara's world. How predictable. The book provided one outcome, and in that outcome your friends would be conveniently on board with the whole thing. I worried: what if they weren't? What would happen if Lucy and Bev exchanged glances and said, *I mean . . . sure, if you feel that way, but it's thirty minutes. It's not like we live on the moon.*

It seemed pretty obvious what would happen: Sara would back down. She'd wish she'd never brought it up. She'd say, *you're right – I'm happy to travel. Half an hour is no trouble at all, really.* Then she would drive home crying, berate herself for failing, and feel even more powerless the next time she saw Lucy and Bev.

I'd returned the *Nice No More* book to my mum's bedside table, baffled. I couldn't see my own attempts paying off like Sara's had – I'd tried, occasionally, to challenge things, but it hadn't worked. It felt like there had been a concrete role assigned for me, an unspoken way of being that I'd adopted as a child and run awkwardly with for years. This role seemed to work for everyone apart from me, so I accepted it. I carried on.

Now Marla's forced my hand – she's pulled the curtain back, brought my niceness out on stage, raw and naked, for everyone to point and laugh at. And if everyone agrees with her, if everyone knows that this has gone on for long enough . . . then something needs to change. *I* need to change.

I pick up one of my art pens, a pale green POSCA, and re-open the A6 sketchpad, ready to give it a new purpose. On the blank first page, I write:

I AM GOING TO STOP BEING SO NICE.

The letters take up the entire page. I stare at them and they stare back at me, curious. *How exactly is this going to happen, do you think?*

I flip to the second page and begin scrawling:

THIS IS HOW IT'S GOING TO HAPPEN ...

Then I put the pen down and realise I have no idea at all.

Google is helpful and unhelpful at the same time. Most of the suggestions seem to come from trained professionals – counsellors and therapists and psychologists – which feels promising but also distant, like they want to help but can't relate. I change up my search, instead looking for 'too nice, need to be more assertive', and find an article that reads like it was put together by a former Anna Campbell. By the time I reach the final sentence, there are tears in my eyes.

I watch a few YouTube videos and make vague pencil notes:

- *No = full sentence. OK to say it.*

- *Boundaries! Set boundaries, keep boundaries. Work out how you want and expect to be treated, what is and isn't OK for you.*

- *Assertive = I win, you win. Not aggressive, not passive. Compromise!*

- *Try to be honest, tell people what you think.*

- *Stop saying sorry all the time.*

- *??*

It feels strange to be doing this. The act of sifting through blog posts and search results has sort of strengthened me, as though each word a stranger has bothered to type on the topic comes with a subtext: *we know you can do something about this.* I keep going, scrolling through page after page of advice. *Self-care. Capacity. Resentful. Addressing your needs.* Some of it makes no sense to me, but I screenshot the stuff that does, jotting down anything particularly noteworthy in the sketchpad.

One recommendation is to set challenges – to try new approaches and hold yourself accountable for giving them a go in practice. *The best way to learn is to do,* says the piece. *So get started with selecting some challenges to test out. What will your first challenge be?* My hand hovers nervously before circling one of my notes, the one about setting boundaries. I read about how everyone is different; how your own boundaries won't ever be the exact same as someone else's; how you need to make them clear. *Maybe you don't like to make plans on weeknights. Maybe you refuse to attend Christmas dinner with your racist uncle. Maybe you tell your sister that it isn't OK for her to borrow clothes without your permission any more.* I read about how some people won't understand your boundaries, how other people will try to bulldoze right through them.

What boundary could you set and keep, starting today? the article asks me.

I turn to a new page.

Challenge One: SETTING A BOUNDARY
If I'm busy or I'm tired, Marla doesn't
come first – I do.

I sit back and take in the sentence, willing my entire being to soak up its message and act accordingly. Then I laugh at how absurd it sounds. I try to imagine myself in action –

ignoring texts, turning down invitations, saying, *I just don't have the energy to listen tonight, Marls – let's talk tomorrow.* I try to imagine Marla's response, whether it'd be anything like the *Nice No More* book, whether she'd pat me on the back for taking steps in this new, non-nice direction if she realised it'd have an impact on her and not just other people. It feels like I already know the answer.

Snapping the sketchpad closed, I say the words out loud. 'Marla doesn't come first – I do. Marla doesn't come first – I do. Marla doesn't come first – *I do.*'

It feels like I'm casting a magic spell. One that might change everything if I manage to get it right.

Eight

The house on Jardine Drive is bigger than I imagined it to be – part of a newish estate with mock Tudor-style beams at the front of each semi-detached home.

Just make it through tonight, I tell myself as I step over a skateboard by the garage, *and you don't have to come back again. Just do the first one, then say something else came up.* I try to think of potential excuses for next Tuesday: a fake emergency, some sort of dad-themed blocker.

A Post-it note next to the doorbell tells me it is 'BROKEN!' and instructs me to 'JUST KNOCK REALLY LOUD INSTEAD'. I smile at the note despite my nerves, and a short woman with long dark hair opens the door like she's been waiting. It makes me jump.

'Hi!' she breathes, gesturing for me to come in with one hand and clutching a stuffed animal with another. 'Anna?' I nod. 'Sorry about that. It's one of those battery-operated things and it never seems to actually work. I've been lurking in the living room to look out for you.'

'Don't worry. You've gone old-school with the knocking – I like it.'

I like *her*, actually, already, despite not wanting to be here. She's wearing a pale pink T-shirt tucked into jeans and her slippers have Bambi on them. One of Bambi's legs is stained with what looks like ketchup. She takes me through the hallway into the kitchen and asks if I want some water or a tea. Their garden is big, and pretty – I peer out of the kitchen window while she runs the tap and makes an excuse for everything being messier than she'd like.

'I don't know how much Jo told you,' Malini begins, and it's funny to hear her refer to Joelle with a nickname I've never known she went by. 'But really, I've . . . I've wanted to learn French for the *longest* time.'

She looks at me for a second, a flicker of what I read as embarrassment on her face, and I smile, as if to say, *continue*.

She does. 'Charlie is four now, so he's not quite as difficult to leave. My other son, Ben, does a great job with him, but the only after-work French class I could find is on a Tuesday, and that's when Ben does his music rehearsal.'

I picture a younger, male version of Malini in some sort of orchestra, playing the trombone and waving to his brother in the crowd.

'Hence . . . me.' I smile again, throwing out my best self-deprecating jazz hands. I regret it instantly but Malini grins back, relaxing.

'Exactly. Ben will always arrive back before me – nine-ish, let's say – so if you're happy for him to come in and take over then, that's what we'll do.'

She's walking around the kitchen now, muttering 'Pen? Pen, pen, pen,' under her breath and putting things into a tote bag that says 'AGAINST ANIMAL TESTING'. Marla has the same one. When Malini finds what she's looking for, she adds it to the bag. Then she whirls back round to face me, her hands clasped together.

'*Now*. Charlie's in bed already. He's normally shattered by seven o'clock and he sleeps right through. But I thought it might be worth you popping in to say hi, in case he does need you at any point. Is that OK?'

'Sure.' I nod, thinking how strange it would be to wake up to a person you'd never seen before eating crisps in your living room. 'Lead the way.'

As we head up the stairs, I side-eye the framed photographs on the wall. Some are clearly from years ago – a Malini who looks no older than twenty has her arms wrapped around a dark-haired man in baggy jeans who is mid-laugh. Further up, there's a much more recent Malini with a baby – Charlie? – on her lap. The dark-haired man seems to have become the no-haired man by this stage. He's in the picture next to her, sitting on the beach with an ice cream melting in one hand.

Malini is telling me more about her evening class while we walk, how she's always wanted to visit Paris, how she can't understand why she's never done it.

'I'm sure you'll get there soon,' I say, and she sighs wistfully.

There's a rustling noise from the bedroom to our left, then silence. We pause outside the door.

'Charlie?' Malini calls, her voice raising in pitch. 'Anna's here. Can I bring her in?'

The rustling starts up again and a child's voice says, 'Yes.'

She pushes the door handle and leads me into a small room, where an even smaller boy lies in bed with a stuffed toy dog. He pulls the covers up over his nose when he sees me, so all I can make out are dark eyes and soft black hair, and I wave.

'Hi, Charlie!'

Charlie sniffs and I realise I'm going to have to do better. I move closer, stepping on to a printed rug by the side of his bed, and kneel down so I'm nearer to his head-height. Malini has perched next to him and is stroking his hair gently. Charlie drops the duvet and picks up the stuffed animal, holding it to his face. He looks so warm and safe.

'I like your dog,' I say, pointing at the toy in his hands. 'What's his name?'

'She's a girl,' Charlie tells me, beaming and leaning forward slightly as he talks. 'She's called Emily.'

Charlie is a better feminist than me and he's only four years old.

'Oh! I'm so sorry. I like Emily a lot. She looks like she goes on adventures with you. Where do you take her?'

He turns Emily around to look at him and smiles, like she's just reminded him. 'Everywhere.'

'We took her to Dartmouth, didn't we? And she came with us when we went to visit *Aachi* in York as well,' prompts Malini, winking at me. She's still clutching the bag and her jacket is on – she tells Charlie that she's going to go and learn some French now, and that when he wakes up, both she and Ben will be back. 'You've had your story, so we'll say goodnight and then Anna's going to come downstairs with me and sit in the living room. That's where you'll be, won't you, Anna?'

I nod. 'All night until Mummy and Ben come home.'

Malini has left me an array of snacks on a tray, which I'd secretly hoped for but didn't want to assume would be a given. So far I've eaten all of the Pringles on offer and started a small bunch of crunchy red grapes. There's a nature documentary playing on the TV – I've stuck with it, willing the mountain goats to safety before the coyotes strike. 'But if the coyotes don't eat this evening,' the narrator tells me, 'they, too, will die.' I shudder and switch channels, rearranging the cherry-red cushions behind me and pulling a blanket over my lap.

Malini's house is modern and beautiful but in a lived-in sort of way – still comfortable to spend time in. I think of Natalie's home, with its expensive-looking artwork on the walls and its 'do-not-touch!' aura – this isn't that. I can see half-used wax crayons on the coffee table and old pairs of trainers by the front door, and almost everywhere looks like it needs to be dusted. I run a finger over the glass table in front of me, outlining a little heart before wiping it away.

There have been no Charlie encounters – I checked on him when I went up to use the bathroom and he was asleep clutching Emily – but several missed messages from Marla. My stomach seizes up at the thought.

Marla 20:49
he was meant to get here at 8:45 but he is 'running late'

Marla 20:52
he has no respect for me or my time. NONE!!

Marla 20:55
oh false alarm he's here

The past couple of days with her have felt odd. With her words from the weekend still hanging in the air and my new boundary at the forefront of my mind, I haven't been sure how to act. I've been trying. But I haven't had the guts to actually bring up what she said at the restaurant, and Marla doesn't seem to have noticed a tension at all. Her texts have popped up as normal, her conversation on the way to sixth form hasn't changed. It's been *me* worrying, overthinking, attempting some kind of forced standoffishness to make a point.

There's sudden movement from outside Malini's house. A key turning in the door. I listen to it swing open and then – after a few seconds – close again very gently, as if to make as little noise as possible. Warm awkwardness floods through me as I become clumsily aware of my presence, like when someone tries to get into a toilet cubicle they don't realise you're using and you don't know if you should say something or just pretend not to exist and hope the lock isn't broken.

I go for the former, leave the sofa, and peer out to the hallway.

The boy on the other side of the door is sitting at the bottom of the stairs, wrestling with a shoe. He glances up when he hears me, points to his foot and says, 'Hi. Sorry. Lace is all knotted. One second.' Then he looks back down and starts to pick at the knot with a fingernail.

'No worries,' I say brightly. 'I'm Anna. I've been looking after Charlie. Are you Ben?' *Are you Ben.* As if he might be another boy who's wandered in off the street.

'Yeah.' Just, *yeah.* He manages to untangle the lace and makes a strangled noise before heaving his shoe off, throwing it to one side, and standing so we're face to face. He smells like outside and his T-shirt is too big for him.

I don't really know what I'm supposed to do at this stage,

but my go-to is *talk*.

'He's been great.' I smile, nodding my head up towards Charlie's room. 'Well, I mean, he's been asleep. But I met him before he went to sleep and he was adorable.'

As I talk, I think. I think that Malini looks too young to be Ben's mum as well as Charlie's – Ben's got to be around my age. I think how strangely impressed and resentful I feel that he can reply *yeah* to my question and not feel the need to cushion that *yeah* with anything else.

Ben glances upstairs, too. 'He's the best. I'm biased, obviously. But also . . . he *is* the best.' He shrugs, then turns and starts walking down the hall towards the kitchen, gently kicking a plastic truck to one side on his way. I'm not sure if I'm expected to follow or not, but he hasn't told me I should and I don't want to intrude, so I stay put and reread the Marla messages, as if staring at them will make them go away. A few moments later, Ben returns with a glass of squash in one hand and a twenty-pound note in the other. He holds out the money towards me.

'This is for you. My mum's still not into the whole online payment thing, so it's cash.'

'Oh! I didn't realise this was paid,' I say, feeling my cheeks burn. 'Thanks.' I take the note and deposit it into the back pocket of my jeans.

He squints at me. 'Were you . . . planning to babysit my brother for free?'

'I— I don't know. Nobody mentioned anything about any money, that's all.'

'I mean, I can take it back, if you don't want it . . . ' I can't work out his expression. He seems almost entertained. Either that or completely baffled.

'No, I do, I j—'

'Sweet. Well, that's you done, then,' he says. I can tell he's ready for me to leave now. 'You back next week?'

I consider it, then nod. 'Sure.'

He does a thumbs-up with a blank face, already turning to scoop up a nearby hoodie and direct his attention to something else. I stand for a second, bewildered, then let myself out.

Marla sends another four messages as I begin the walk home, all additions to her ignored soliloquy from earlier. They buzz in my hand, hurried and demanding, the kind we both know are designed for an instant response.

Marla 21:07
all fine, food is on the way

Marla 21:07
what should we watch, donnie darko
or american beauty???

Marla 21:07

i say american beauty and we cannot agree so
YOU are the decider here AC

Marla 21:07

quick quick cast your vote

Set the boundary, keep the boundary. Set the boundary, keep the boundary, I think, retrieving the niceness notebook from my bag:

> *If I'm busy or I'm tired,*
> *Marla doesn't come first — I do.*

I *am* tired. I'm exhausted, but any bravery from before has faded away now, leaving behind a bleak reality: I'm out of my depth, and not the kind of person who could ever ignore seven messages in a row, especially when they come from Marla.

I reply, same as always. I tell her what she wants to hear.

After that, I tell myself what *I* want to hear: that these things take time, that you can always start them tomorrow instead of today. Then I crawl into bed, defeated.

Nine

'Oh, I forgot – Joelle wants to know how it went. The babysitting.'

We're sitting on a bench outside the science block and Marla is plaiting a tiny bit at the front of her hair like some sort of elf princess. It's colder than I expected – *summer is dead,* Marla proclaimed to the world this morning, *and now September is sitting on its corpse.*

'It was actually fine,' I say, waving at Ryan as he walks past us mid-phone call. He waves back without energy. 'Malini's son Charlie is super-cute and very sleepy, so I literally got paid to eat her kitchen supplies and watch Netflix. No complaints.'

There weren't, really – apart from maybe Ben. Considering how much internal angst the process of signing up for babysitting caused me, the babysitting itself was relatively stress-free. *Maybe next time I could take a sketchbook,* I think.

'I'll report back,' says Marla drily. 'Joelle kept asking about it. I swear this is the friend whose husband walked out a few years ago or something. Was there a Mr Malini?'

The photos from the stairs come back to me – the young dark-haired man with the jeans, and the years-later version of him with Charlie as a baby – and I try to remember any hints Malini might have given me in the few minutes we spent together. Marla looks at me expectantly and I shake my head.

'No, not that she mentioned. She has another son, though. Ben. Probably our age.'

'Yeah, he's Year 13 too, I think. I haven't met him.' Marla yawns. The plait is finished. She digs around in her bag for a hair tie, eventually fishing out a large red one that looks like it's seen better days.

I'm glad we're talking about something neutral, something that doesn't leave me needing to think too hard about how I speak to her.

'He's fine,' I say. 'He's . . . indifferent.'

'What d'you mean?'

'I don't know, really. Quiet, maybe. He seemed sort of . . . blah.'

I'm still not completely sure what it was about Ben that did bother me. I can't pinpoint it. He wasn't rude, exactly. And *quiet* isn't the right word. All he needed to do was come home and pay me, and he did that, and then I left. But I was surprised by how apathetic he seemed, like he didn't care if I warmed to him or not. Like there wasn't anything specific he wanted strangers to think.

Marla throws her head back, mock-exasperated. 'I don't know what *blah* means. Specifics, please, AC. Paint a picture for me.'

'Specifics like . . . one-word answers. I asked him if he was Ben and he just said "yeah". Don't you think that's weird?'

'No. Who else would he have been? Sounds like a dumb thing to ask. Oh my *god.*' Marla stops and claps her hands together. 'Was he pretty?'

The question makes me laugh, despite everything. 'I guess. Malini said he had some music rehearsal, and I thought she meant, like, a brass quartet. But he looked more . . . practise-in-the-garage-with-an-old-guitar.'

'Well. He *sounds* pretty.' She winks at me jokingly.

'I'm sorry – is this not the kind of thing you would *hate* Carl for saying?' I tease, poking her in a rib. Her face immediately falls and she tugs at the hairband holding its elvish plait in place. The ends unfurl and the remainder of her work hangs, lifeless.

'Oh, *Marls,*' I say. 'I didn't mean it like that – I was joking.' Her comment had felt so throwaway that I'd wanted to commemorate it, to reassure her that Carl's equivalents might mean exactly the same.

Carl and I have met a few times now, mostly at events that Marla's invited me to. He's tall and solid, and when he puts his arm around Marla she becomes tinier than ever, a block-fringed pixie. He looks at her like she invented life.

Marla always says that the nicest thing that ever happened to her was when she and Carl started speaking at the same time once and interrupted each other, and he said, *sorry, what did you want to say?* and she said, *it wasn't important,* and Carl said, *no, everything you have to say is important.* He wasn't even trying to be impressive. He didn't know Marla would tell the story afterwards. He just said it, and then waited for her to speak.

I guess what I mean by all of that is: Carl doesn't come across as someone who is likely to run off with a girl from a Year 10 school trip he's been secretly messaging declarations of love to. He really does not. But Marla's mind is never resting – and it's Carl at the moment, but I feel like she might have this problem with anyone she loved.

A few weeks ago, I overheard Aleks and Natalie talking about it in the common room. Aleks was like, *it's ridiculous; she planned their entire break-up last week because he did two hearts on his goodnight message instead of three,* and Natalie nodded. *I feel bad for her, but I still don't get it. If she doesn't calm down, he'll just get sick of her anyway.*

I didn't tell Marla they'd said that, obviously. She probably knows it's ridiculous. You can know something is illogical or unreasonable and still feel it, though, which is the strangest thing about brains. Like those times when you figure out that you're snappy because you're tired, but that knowledge doesn't automatically get rid of your snappiness. Or when you know you're only happy because you got a message from the person you wanted a message from, and the sensible part of your brain is saying, *this feeling is fickle and temporary,* but another part is saying, *I will never, ever be sad again.*

I remember Marla saying that she would never, ever be happy again. It was last June, and we were in the park on one of those evenings where it's been so hot all day that it still feels steamy at night, and if you shut your eyes it's like you're in a warm country far away from England. Marla had told me all about it, how her dad had been *seeing* someone from his job, how her mum hadn't known, how now her mum did know but had said, *Marla, listen, we will work through this.*

It was odd, because I'd never heard of families *working through* things like that. I'd only ever seen affairs in films and TV shows, and they'd always ended in divorce, which made sense to me. Marla told me that Joelle had suspected for months, which didn't make sense to me.

'How can you carry on *living* with someone and not mention it?' Marla had asked as we lay on the grass together, holding hands like it would make things better. 'How could you even function? Why would you be happy to carry on eating spaghetti fucking bolognese with someone who may or may not be having sex with Jenny from Finance?'

I told her I didn't know.

When I was at Marla's house a few weeks afterwards, we were all sitting in the kitchen, which is the biggest room in their house. Marla's dad, Mr Mackinlay – or Don, if you like him, but I don't – was out buying compost or something with Marla's younger brother, Leo, and I was on my phone, and I was aware that Marla and Joelle were talking quietly but I'd zoned out and wasn't really listening any more. Then suddenly Marla had thrown her plate across the room so it smashed on the kitchen floor, and she was shouting, shouting, *why would you forgive this?*

Joelle said, *things are complicated, it's never as simple as you think, darling, never,* and Marla said, *you're worse than him; you're a pushover. You let it happen.* Then she started to sob, loud and desperate, like a child who's just hit the floor in the playground. I found a shard of plate in my bag the next day.

She's sniffing now, not quite crying but almost there. I shuffle along the bench, moving closer to her, sensing she's ready to speak. The red hair tie is still in her hand and she's picking at it, pulling it back and then letting it go so the elastic flicks gently across her skin. 'He just doesn't ev–'

A shadow appears in front of us, and we both look up to see Ryan. Marla bristles instantly, her almost-tears pushed to one side, and says, 'So. Tell me more about the *actual* child you are babysitting, not his nerdy brother.'

Ryan looks confused. He's clutching a new metal bottle in one hand – courtesy of Aleks – and his face is slightly sweaty, like he's been busy. 'You've been babysitting?'

'I–'

'She has,' interrupts Marla, in a superior voice. 'And I am just hearing about it now.'

This is Marla-speak for *so leave us alone*, but Ryan either doesn't pick up on the vibe or chooses to ignore it. He wasn't around for lunch today. I'd hoped this had meant things had got better for him – that he'd joined a midweek sports team or started to find other, more exciting acquaintances to spend time with – but the phone call and the distracted air around him tell me that's not true. He throws himself down next to us on the bench and I talk more about Charlie and his feminist soft toy collection.

'All very cute. I will tell Joelle,' says Marla. She is a much better actor than me, when she wants to be.

Ryan looks perplexed. 'Do you always call your mum by her first name?'

She scowls. 'Yes. *Or* you can just tell her yourself, AC, if you want to come round later. We're having lasagne. Plus . . . we never got to finish our *chat*.' Her eyes flit over to Ryan. He yawns, unbothered. 'So I need you.'

Time speeds up when people need me.

'OK,' I say. 'Lasagne. Sounds good.'

Technically, this isn't another failed attempt at challenge one, because I'm neither busy nor tired. But I don't even know if that makes things better. There don't seem to be any rules in place about how to deal with simply . . . not wanting to. What happens if I'd prefer to go home and watch TV or try out my new acrylic paint set? Who determines the outcome in a situation like that?

She gets up, stretches, starts to walk away as the bell rings to signal the beginning of the afternoon. 'Nice. I'll ask Joelle if you can stop over.'

The message is clear to me: *Marla does.*

Ten

Ryan disappears again on Monday.

I don't mention it to Marla because I'm scared she'll make some comment I don't want to hear, but my attention bounces around the common room during our free period, ears responding every time the door opens.

Natalie picks up on it. 'Do you think you should text him?' she asks as we hug on Tuesday morning, after I tell her that Ryan is still nowhere to be seen. There's a book in her hand with a blueish tree on its cover, and a half-eaten apple on the seat next to her. 'Maybe it's to do with his dad.'

Despite my hazy concerns, I never pressed Ryan for extra information when he ignored my question about his dad a couple of weeks ago. It had felt nosy, so I hadn't mentioned it again, but it had stayed in the back of my mind, a distant worry.

'I don't actually know,' I tell her. 'We didn't speak over the weekend – I probably *should* see how he's doing.' She nods and returns to her book.

I type out a message at lunchtime, editing the sentences several times in an effort to sound natural; nothing scandalous, just a new friend checking in. There's a chance I'm crossing a line, but even before I became the designated Broadacre Buddy it always felt like my job to help with things like this. To notice an off-day, to read between the lines of whatever was being presented and say, *I see you. I see you. You aren't on your own.* Nobody else ever seemed to do that. Not for other people, and definitely not for me.

Ryan 13:28
Just needed to lay low for a bit

Ryan 13:33
Am not good over text, can we speak face to face when Im back? Need to talk to someone

Anna 13:38
of course we can. really hope you're OK ryan

What does he need to talk about? Why would he need to *lay low*? The phrase seems like movie-talk, worlds away from something the rest of my friends would come out with. There are too many gaps to fill, too many unknowns to figure out, and they all make me nervous.

Malini dashes out with a wholesome *au revoir, ma chérie!* this week, leaving me with a plate of biscuits and a parting film recommendation of *When Harry Met Sally*. 'I promise you – it's the rom-com to end all rom-coms, Anna.'

She isn't wrong. It keeps me company while I crunch through biscuits and doodle Meg Ryan with her fluffy hair and giant knitted jumpers. As the credits roll, I'm seriously considering if a cropped 80s perm could be a viable option for me. Maybe Aleks will have opinions.

I wasn't anxious to babysit this week – to chat to Malini, or be on call for Charlie – but as it nears 9 p.m. the thought of seeing Ben again is leaving me on edge and I'm not sure why. I stand up, shake my arms, take a little walk around the living room. There's a mirror on the opposite wall, just to the right of the TV, and I get up and hover in front of it for a while, as though I expect something to happen. I smile at the mirror without opening my mouth. It looks insincere, the sort of smile you'd receive from a middle-aged woman who didn't mean it. I add teeth to the mix. Too much. Too friendly, too generous. Then straight-faced, blank-line lips. Frown. I wonder what I look like when I get angry. I don't think I've showed anyone any anger since I was a child who could get away with it.

His keys in the door make me jump. I dash back to the sofa, placing my sketches back on to the central coffee table and trying to look semi-occupied, instead of a keen dog waiting for its owner to arrive home. I'm balling up a biscuit wrapper in my hand as Ben walks in, and I wave with it, my hand a silly fist.

'Hi.'

I don't bother smiling, because smiling's for nice people and I don't feel like he'll care either way. Ben offers me his own version of a grin, which is more of an eye-widen and brow-raise with the very corners of his mouth following suit out of obligation. He's wearing the same giant black T-shirt as last week. It says CONVERGE on it in big letters. I think, *I will Google that later.*

'Hey. All good with Charlie?'

I nod at him. 'He's been sleeping all night, no problems at all. I'm not sure you *should* be paying me, really.' Take my bad conversation, Ben. Take it and let me be on my way.

'Mm. Does seem kind of suspect that *I* don't get any twenties when I do this.' He grimaces, and it takes me a second to realise he's joking. A teeth-smile materialises involuntarily.

Maybe I misread him, I think. I decide to try again, to get beyond the apathy of last week, so I ask about his music rehearsal and he laughs. 'My mum always calls it that. It's just band practice – I play the drums.' He shows me a bright red blister on the side of an index finger.

'Oh, wow,' I say, partly to the news and partly to the blister. 'Are you any good?'

'You mean me personally, or the band itself?'

I think about it and shrug. 'Both?'

'No.' He pauses for a second, deadpan, and I let a snort of baffled amusement escape from the back of my nose. He's as blasé as last week but there's something about it that feels warmer to me now.

I start to pack my things away, ready to leave on a better note this time. My empty tea mug gets placed on to the tray from Malini's kitchen, the one with painted chickens all over it. There are still a few biscuits on the matching plate – I gesture towards them and Ben says, 'absolutely,' before taking two.

'What do you do when you're here?' he asks as he chews. 'You can set up Mario Kart if you want. Charlie is all about that game.'

'Thanks,' I tell him, shoving my pencil case into a side-pocket. 'I just draw, really. It's nice to have the time to myself.'

'Spoken like a fellow older sibling,' he says, and it takes me a second to work out what he means.

'Oh! No – I don't actually have any brothers or sisters. I have . . .'

I trail off, unsure of how to finish the sentence. *I have a dad who's forgotten how to function. I have a terrible habit of neglecting myself. I have a Marla.*

Ben seems to read my hesitance to extend this part of the conversation. Instead, he nods at the open sketchpad on its way to my bag. 'Who's that?'

'This? They're my friends. It's only rough stuff – I like copying photos off my phone.'

It's a quick pen-drawing of the three of them – Marla on the left, her red heart-shaped sunglasses dominating her face, with Natalie and Aleks in the background, ugly-laughing at something one of them has just said. The original picture is from over the summer, when we all went to London for the day.

Ben takes the sketchpad from me with his biscuit-free hand. 'This is awesome. Who's who?'

I always get shy when people compliment my work, but I point at the drawing, happy to tilt our focus over to the people in it. 'Marla, with the heart eyes, she's the main one. And then the other two are Aleks and Natalie.'

The main one. I hate that I called Marla that, like the rest of us are her metaphorical backing singers.

As Ben passes the book back to me, my phone lights up on the coffee table.

Missed calls: Marla (7)

Speak of the devil, as my grandma always used to say. But seven missed calls is a lot, even for Marla. *Maybe something awful has happened,* I think. *Or maybe it hasn't, and she's just phoning the nice girl because nobody else will answer.* She calls again as I'm considering this possibility, and her name on the screen throws me.

'I'm sorry,' I say, snapping back to life. I rearrange my face into an apologetic smile for Ben's benefit and awkwardly show him the phone I've just grabbed from the table. 'She's called a lot. I should just check my friend is all right.'

He nods, like, *yes, of course,* and I accept the eighth call as I pace out of Malini's living room, hearing Ben gently close the door behind me. Marla speaks before I have chance to. Her voice is jagged and sweaty, as if I've caught her in the middle of a run. I ask if she's OK.

She sniffs, and I know what's coming. 'No. It's *Carl.* He's . . . he ended it, AC. He dropped off the food and then he said he wouldn't be staying because he doesn't have the *energy* any more. He came out with all this stuff about how *no one can really love you until you love yourself,* all this patronising live/laugh/ love shit. And now I'm sitting here with a cold takeaway and . . .' Another sob. 'It's done. Carl's gone.'

Within seconds I'm ready – jacket on, feet stuffed into shoes, excuses prepared. I've promised to head over to Marla's right now, right this second, to sit with her for as long as she needs. I feel like a paramedic.

Ben knocks on the other side of the living room door, gentle but still loud enough to let me know he's there. 'Can . . . can I come out?'

'Of course! I'm sorry. I didn't mean to trap you in your own house.'

He smiles – the eye-widen and brow-raise thing, really – as he walks into the hall. 'Everything OK?'

'Fine, thanks,' I tell him, moving past him to collect my bag. Someone has sped up my heart. 'I need to go, but I am absolutely fine.'

As I jog over to Marla's house, phone in hand, I wonder if this is another failure to tick off the first challenge. I keep trying, I keep thinking about my boundary but then running in the opposite direction for Marla again every time she needs it. Is that bad?

She's waiting at her bedroom window when I step on to the driveway, her face pink and puffy, and she waves with her tissue like a war widow. *No,* I tell myself. *This is different.* I hear her fiddling with the front-door lock, shouting something to her mum about *Anna* and *an emergency,* and I brace myself to be a good friend.

Eleven

'Look. Ryan's back.'

Natalie prods me in the shoulder and uses her brows as urgent arrows, directing me to the form-room door that Ryan's now walking through. He ambles in late, nods at Miss James, who nods back like they have a secret language, and then takes the only available seat, rows away from us. I swivel back to catch his eye – to look at him in a way that says, *where* were *you?* – and he mouths something I can't work out.

Marla doesn't notice Ryan walk in. She's staring at a fingernail she's been attacking for the last few minutes – there doesn't look enough left to bite any more but she finds a piece to tear off anyway, gnawing at it in an animalistic way. It makes me shudder. Joelle is not a *skip class because you're sad about your break-up* kind of parent but I'm confident that if anyone could have done with a day off today, it's Marla. After I left her house she sent frantic messages throughout the night, the final one at 3 a.m., and yet here she is five hours later, pretending to be fine because she has to.

We meet up with Aleks and Natalie at lunch like usual, the four of us silently returning to our new arrangement of five when Ryan joins us. I wonder if Ryan thinks I'm too nice. I wonder if he goes home every day and says, *god, Mum, that Anna girl tries too hard*, and his mum says, *give it time, love, you'll have some proper friends soon*.

I'm not sure. He's a new breed of pale today. There are grey, swollen pouches under his eyes and he doesn't seem completely present, as though his thoughts are swimming outside of his head somewhere and he needs slightly longer than normal to gain access to them. Marla, head down, engrossed in a salad she isn't eating, has exactly the same vibe. I glance to my left, then to my right, then sigh very gently so no one can hear.

Aleks addresses the largest elephant in the room first. 'How are you doing, Marls?'

Marla looks up from her food. 'Fine.' There's talent in how little emotion she manages to convey in that one word. It's at a complete zero.

I can tell Aleks didn't receive the response she was expecting. She falters for a moment and then jumps back in, smiling kindly. 'Oh. Well, that's good. I know it's shit but I think it's probably for the best, overall. From what you've said, anyway.'

She holds Marla's gaze for a second and then takes a bite

of baked potato, as if to indicate a return to business as usual. Awkward check-in complete. Job done. She won't mean any malice with it – it's just that if someone tells Aleks they're fine, then they're fine. She doesn't do subtext.

Marla pulls a face I've seen before, her eyebrows springing to life. '*What?*'

Aleks glances up mid-mouthful, clearly surprised. 'What?'

'I would like to know what you mean,' says Marla, monotone again, no blinking.

Natalie swallows loudly. 'I think—'

It's not often she jumps in to translate for Aleks like this, to water down a message like I would, and Aleks looks hurt by the action. She interrupts Natalie, glaring.

'What I mean is what I just *said* – that it's probably for the best. I'm not saying it's not rubbish – I know it's rubbish, Marls – but you've been up and down about Carl loads recently. You know you have. Is it not better to end it and actually be happy?'

The point is clear and fair, well-intended, but not needed today. It's too early for Marla to hear it. *Stop*, I try to magically communicate to Aleks. *I know you mean good things, but this is a conversation we need to have another time.*

'You would think,' says Marla wearily, 'but you'd be wrong. You don't know Carl, you don't know our relationship. None of this is *better*.'

She picks up her bag, swings it over one shoulder and storms out of the cafeteria. A Year 11 boy near the entrance shouts 'wheyyyy', wanting attention from the girl in distress, and she looks at him like she'll turn him to stone.

It isn't until the end of the day – art, my final Wednesday period – that Ryan and I actually get a chance to talk. The old rickety classroom – full of students and movement – is a good place to camouflage yourself for a difficult conversation, I decide. He nods at me as he sits down and I return the greeting with a wave.

There's a strange clumsiness to our relationship – for all of Marla's snippiness at Niccolo's, she wasn't completely wrong with her analysis of Ryan's place in the group. When he *is* at sixth form he'll wander over to sit with us, sometimes distantly polite, other times listening intently to whatever's being discussed that day. He brings in books I've never heard of for Natalie, all sad-sounding men and battered old front covers. He nods sincerely when Aleks tells us about recycling myths, when Marla asks if her hair looks OK. But he still doesn't share much out loud. It's like he's happy to be a background feature, an offline version of the person who reads every message in the group chat but rarely responds. *He might not feel comfortable telling four girls about his personal life,* I remind myself. *He's sharing little bits with me. Maybe that's all he can handle right now.*

He picks up a pencil, and I start small. 'How was your weekend?'

'Good.' He blinks after he says it. 'Actually, bad. I don't know why I said that.'

That's one thing we have in common, I think. *We both say something's good when it isn't.*

'Were you ill?' I ask, giving him the opportunity to duck out of this one if he wants to. He's still not looking particularly healthy – the grey hue to his skin has persisted throughout the day. But he said he was *laying low,* like there was something – or someone – he was trying to avoid. He must remember he told me that.

He's quiet for a few seconds. I listen to the murmurs bouncing around the tables, the fuzzy radio in the corner by the door, the rain on the ancient roof above us. Ryan acts like he's engrossed in his sketchbook, continuing the shading on a pencil drawing. I tilt my head to look at it properly and see a man with flame-tattooed arms screaming into a microphone, realistic like a photograph.

Ryan clears his throat. 'We left. We left Liverpool because we had to leave, and we didn't want him to find us, but he did.'

I don't say anything, because I don't think I need to yet.

'And we thought it'd be OK, because this is so far away from Liverpool – like, it's not as if he can just jump on a bus and pop in for tea, is it. We thought he would leave us alone. But apparently . . . men like him don't really do that. So he showed up at the house a couple of weeks ago. I think he'd driven past a few times to make sure we were there. He doesn't like my grandad – he's a bit scared of him, I think – but my grandad went out on that Thursday night, so . . . '

He shrugs at me, turning back to his drawing and pulling a face that says, *well, you know the rest. What can you do?*

'Did he come back this week?' I ask cautiously, afraid to hear the answer. His words drip slowly through my mind, each one laced with something darker.

'Sunday. He waited 'til my mum was outside emptying the bins. Just appeared, and then he came out with the same stuff: "I made a mistake! It won't be like that any more!" All the standard excuses we've heard before. Then when she told him to go, he wouldn't, and she ran back into the house and he banged on the door and was like, "you fucking bitch, Helen". I think he waited outside for about half an hour – I was looking out from the bathroom upstairs and my sister was asleep, but we'd called my grandad, so as soon as he came home my dad just . . . went.'

There's a strange ringing in my ears now. I screw up my nose to try and ease it and wonder if the conclusion I've just reached in my mind is correct.

'How . . . how's your mum?' It's a puny question, but it's the best I can do.

'She's a mess. And Vicky – that's my sister – refuses to sleep now. And I just couldn't face being here. So then that made it worse, 'cause my mum got all weird about "missing out on learning" and . . . I dunno. My brain's too full for any of that. Now he knows where we are, he'll be back.'

My heart hurts for him. I say, 'oh, Ryan.' I think back to Mr Bains on the first day and the way he told me I'd be showing Ryan the ropes, helping him from lesson to lesson. Why didn't he warn me? Why didn't he mention anything about this?

Ryan keeps his eyes on the paper and I dip my dried-out paintbrush into water, swirling it around at the bottom of the jar and watching as the colours dance together. Then I bring it up to the air for a moment, drenched and heavy, gasping for breath.

Twelve

We still talk about Carl every day. About his new haircut. About his dog. About his cryptically worded Instagram caption, which may or may not have been a reference to Marla. About whether maybe, potentially, *eventually*, he might reconsider his decision. But after the face-off with Aleks last week, Marla seems less keen than ever to take these conversations outside our bubble of two.

'Nobody gets it,' she says suddenly, as we're walking to sixth form on Monday. 'I don't know *anyone* who's been in this situation. Aleks thinks she's some sort of relationship oracle because she's been with Leah for a million years, but she doesn't know shit.'

It burns a bit to be told that I don't understand. I don't, really – boys have never affected me like they have Marla. I've *liked* them, I guess, but I haven't spent my spare time wondering where they are, or what they're doing, or who they're speaking to. When things have fizzled out, I haven't cried myself to sleep. In some ways, I realise, the only overwhelming emotion I've felt has been relief.

Marla glances at me like she's just cottoned on to what came out of her mouth. 'Sorry, AC. You know I don't mean you.'

She calls me in the evenings, most days, and I'm ready and waiting each time, armed with excuses to neglect the first challenge, poised to dispense the same few lines. It's become a habit, and a habit is hard to give up. *Oh, no. Yeah, totally. But he seemed like he cared about you loads, Marls, so— Yeah, maybe you could speak to him in a month, or something. Mm. Becky lives in Scotland, though, you said, so why would he break up with you for someone who lives in Scotland? No, I don't think you're crazy. No. What? No, I didn't mean he would leave you for someone who lives nearby. He— Oh, sorry, you go. Mm. Yeah, tell me.*

Sometimes she messages me afterwards:

i love you so much

I read it and I think, *maybe this is just what friendship is. You work through things together until you are blue in the face because that is what you have to do.* I try to tell myself that boundaries might not even count for this sort of thing, that if someone means that much to you then they mean that much forever, even when the thought of hearing their voice starts to make you inexplicably sad. Other times, I hang up so drained of energy that I put my face against the bedroom wall just to feel the coolness of it and don't speak for the rest of the evening.

My resources are depleted from other angles, too. As I curl up on Monday night, ready to begin tackling my first art project of the year, my pocket buzzes again:

Ryan 20:34
Hows your art going? Have you decided what subject to do?

We've been given a list of topics for this first coursework project. Stuff like 'Time and Space' or 'Food and Drink' or 'Structure'. Starting points. *Stimuli*, Mrs Gana always calls them.

I showed the list to my dad at the breakfast table this morning, knowing he's usually good for an artist recommendation, and he nodded eagerly before pulling out a book called *Dada and Surrealism*. I skim through it now as I sit, bookmarking pages of interest.

I'm one of those people who likes to give this this sort of thing some thought. I'll narrow it down to two or three suggestions, then jot down a bunch of ideas using an old sketchpad I don't mind getting scribbles in. When something jumps out, when I suddenly think, *yeah, that could work*, I'll start Googling artists who come to mind – Bridget Riley or Raoul Hausmann or David Hockney – and see where that takes me. I really love

David Hockney. He has a painting called *A Bigger Splash*, which I feel like most people have seen at some point or another, and every time I look at it it's like someone has spring-cleaned my brain and taken the bits I don't need any more to a charity shop. I think I'll want it on my wall one day.

> **Anna 20:38**
> just starting work on it now! no solid ideas yet though so we'll see . . .

> **Anna 20:39**
> how's yours coming along?

> **Ryan 20:53**
> Not exactly full of ideas either to be honest. My dad got hold of my mum's details at the weekend. Dont know how, probably one of her friends caved. But she had 97 missed calls off him and a load of other stuff

I close my sketchbook, alarmed, and re-read Ryan's latest message. It takes me a few minutes to type out a reply – I backspace *so sorry* and *really scary for you*, settling on what I hope is some more helpful, optimistic wording. He responds right away and we send hurried messages back and forth for an hour, ping-ping-ping-ping-ping. *Do any of his friends back in Liverpool know about this,* I wonder, as I return the unused sketchbook to my bag. *Would any of them help?*

10 p.m. I rub my eyes with both fists, the way babies do, and make a silent promise to start work on the art project soon. Ryan is struggling, he needs *someone*, but I can do both. Not all of my time is for other people. I'll claw some back, leave my phone in another room for the night, make a start. A week is a long time.

Thirteen

I'm settled delicately on Malini's sofa – torso straight, not yet allowing myself to sprawl out comfortably – with my niceness notebook open in one hand and the TV on quietly in the background for company. I haven't bothered to change the channel, so it's some old sitcom I couldn't name. The canned laughter is getting on my nerves.

Challenge One: SETTING A BOUNDARY
If I'm busy or I'm tired, Marla doesn't
come first – I do.

'Ha,' I say out loud, positive I won't be able to produce any examples of when I *have* actually come first over the last few weeks. It feels as if every opportunity I've had – every moment I've assessed as a new chance to try – has somehow led to nothing. My handwritten notes prove it:

Difficult. Makes sense in theory, like
everything else, but how are you supposed
to ignore your best friend when she's sad??

Failed today. Went to Marla's and talked
about Carl for three and a half hours.
What if I had a problem? When would
we talk about that?

Don't understand how this works.
WILL NEVER UNDERSTAND
HOW THIS WORKS.

The book in my palm suddenly feels like a physical reminder of my lack of progress. My lack of power. I slam it down onto the sofa next to me, exasperated. I want to call up the experts, whoever they are, and ask them, *how do you stick to this? How do you keep any kind of boundary when your entire personality has always been based around having none?*

The sitcom has finished but the next episode has started and I don't have the energy for anything else so I stick with it, scrolling through what I've missed on my phone at the same time, my attention never fully resting on either. Just before 9 p.m., the front door swings open. Ben. I lock my phone and walk out to meet him.

'Hey,' he says. He does an exaggerated shake to show how

cold it is. I say, 'brrr,' in agreement, and he smiles.

His good mood from last week has remained and I'm glad about it, if only because mine hasn't. We stand in the doorway of the living room for a few minutes while he tells me about band practice, and I ask about the sixth form he goes to, which turns out to be the same as Carl's. I show him a photo of Carl that Marla took at her birthday party in July and he shakes his head. 'Nope, don't know him. There's, like, a thousand students, though.'

'What happened last week, by the way?' he asks, taking his coat off and folding it on to a reading chair by the window. 'You got those phone calls from your friend and then it all sounded a bit full-on. Did it turn out OK in the end? Is *she* OK?'

'Oh,' I say, remembering the way I left his house: full emergency mode. 'Yeah. Well, no, not really. What happened last week was that my friend Marla's boyfriend – that Carl guy from your sixth form – broke up with her.' I frown, to show it's still fresh.

'Ouch. Poor Marla. She must've needed you.'

'Mm,' I say. 'That's why I rushed off so quickly. She was *so* upset. And she still thinks there might be hope for them – her and her ex, I mean – but realistically . . . I don't know. I think he loved her a lot but . . . he sounded kind of done.'

Ben frowns in return and makes a *bleugh* noise. 'There's never really a good way to try and tell someone that. Isn't she the one with the sunglasses on from your drawing?'

'Yep. No one forgets Marla.' I laugh as I say it, but the words sound bleak and bitter. He looks puzzled, a crinkle appearing in the gap between his eyebrows, and I shrivel up at the possibility that I've said too much. 'It's fine. She's just . . . a lot at the moment. It's a really long story.'

'Well, I *love* a long story,' says Ben, gesturing to the family bookcase in the corner of the room. I turn around and see a stash of well-thumbed *Lord of the Rings* books on the middle shelf. He isn't lying and he doesn't seem like a gossip and maybe it *would* be a good idea for me to run all of this past another living human being before I scream.

'Huh. I only ever managed to read *The Hobbit*,' I say, more to change the subject than anything else.

Ben takes the bait, moving over to the sofa. 'What? That's outrageous. You've seen all the films, though, right? Please tell me you've seen the films, Anna.'

There is a *Fellowship of the Ring* poster that's been on my bedroom wall since 2012. Until a couple of years ago, I would offer a covert smile to tall, elderly-looking trees, just in case there was a grain of truth in the concept of Ents. 'Of course. A lot. And the other books are on my list, I promise. I'm just not a big reader. Though I did get through *The Hobbit*. I loved it, but it made me sad.'

'It made you sad? Oh, but it's so hopeful! Like, I get you, but surely the thing about *The Hobbit* is th—' says Ben, but then he stops. Reaches under one leg. The niceness notebook emerges in his hand, and I practically retch.

'That's mine!' I say, reaching to snatch the book from him, but there's no point because it's open and he's seen it and he knows what it says:

I AM GOING TO STOP BEING SO NICE.

We both stare at the green words like we've just discovered a dead body together.

'Sorry,' Ben says, and I can tell that he means it, that he knows he's intruded on something he shouldn't have had access to. He closes the book and slides it back on to the coffee table, his movements extra-careful. I sigh, half-mortified, half-exhausted.

You have to explain things like this, I always think, if only because saying nothing makes you look even stranger than the truth would. And I don't know Ben, not really. I can tell him the outlines of this – the vague plans I have to tick off these challenges, knowing it'll be a miracle if I actually do – and then . . . never mention it again. It's not like he's going to care enough to ask for a progress report next Tuesday.

'I'm sort of . . . I'm just trying to *work* on myself,' I mutter, echoing the new language I've heard from people online. 'Like . . . boundary-setting. Not being so nice all the time. That kind of stuff.' It comes out more gruff and defensive than I mean it to.

Ben raises his eyebrows. 'Jeez. Well, good for you.'

Job done.

'Thanks,' I say, getting up to leave. I pick up the book and wrap my fingers around it, tight like a lock. 'Hopefully it'll help.'

'What do you need it to help?' asks Ben, and I swivel round to look at him, surprised. He bites his lip. 'I mean, like ... what's the problem here?'

'Oh my god, there are so many problems,' I tell him, continuing to clear my things away in a manner I hope comes off as nonchalant. He looks bewildered, like he can't possibly imagine why the talkative girl who babysits his brother on a Tuesday evening would need to write block-capital declarations about her behaviour going forward.

'Yeah, but what?'

I don't think he's prying. I think he might actually want to know. So I tell him. I tell him about Ryan, about what Marla said, about the niceness notebook, and he listens, he actually listens, and when I'm done he says, 'Wow.'

I say, 'Yeah, wow,' but nervously, because I'm not sure if he's being sarcastic or not.

He's still sitting in the same place on the sofa, but one knee is tucked up under his chin now, arms wrapped around his leg like it'll help him to think. 'I feel like there's quite a lot to unpack here.'

Standing on the living room rug with the notebook in one hand, I wait for him to start the unpacking. *Tell me what you think of me, Ben. Pile on and remind me how unnecessarily nice I am.*

'Well. Obviously, you said you'd look after this Ryan guy even though you didn't want to. That was kind of you, but yeah, your best friend called you out on it in a pretty brutal way and you didn't manage to tell her it bothered you. And it sounds like you've probably been sitting on all this since then, as well as worrying about being there for Ryan *and* helping Marla – Marla? – when she needs it. Right?'

He shrinks back as I process his words. They bounce around the living room, jarring and raw, making contact with my skin every so often. I twitch.

'I could be way off,' says Ben, his face concerned. 'I don't know you very well, and—'

'No,' I interrupt, 'You're actually spot-on. And the worst part is that I *know* how stupid it sounds. If you told me another person acted that way, I'd . . . I'd think . . . ' I pause, exasperated. 'It's like, why would you be like that? Why would a person be like that? But I'm so used to it now, and everyone else is so used to it, too, that . . . I don't know. It's endless. And I'd love to be one of those girls who just speaks her mind and doesn't care and everyone says, "oh, what you see is what you get!" – but I can't. It's always been like this. It doesn't work when I try to do it any differently.'

'But . . . it could. That's why you've written that down, right?' He gestures loosely towards my hands.

'I guess. I don't know where my cut-off is or what I'm even like without this, sometimes, and that scares me. So I need to try it. I've started setting myself these challenges – that's why the notebook exists,' I say, waving it foolishly. 'But I've already failed at the first one. So . . . '

'It doesn't matter if you messed up the first challenge. There's a lot of pages in that book.' He's smiling, and it helps. 'Maybe you can start again. Forget challenge one – what's challenge two?'

I open it back up again, flipping through the pages for inspiration.

'Maybe . . . maybe *honesty*?' I say, the word feeling foreign in my mouth. 'One of the suggestions I wrote down was to try to be honest with people. Tell them when I'm upset. Tell them what I actually think, instead of what I *think* I should think. And I know it might not work, but I've got to try. I can't be like this forever.'

My voice cracks on the last sentence and the tears I'd kept lodged away somewhere finally bleed out.

Ben looks at me with kind eyes, calm, like he sees this sort of thing all the time. 'You won't be like this forever. Not if you don't want to be.'

I sniff, rooting around in a coat pocket. There's a half-used packet of tissues in there and I tweeze one out, walking over to the mirror to dab at the soft skin under my eyes. 'I don't want to be.' The girl in the reflection glowers again. '*I don't want to be.*'

Fourteen

Ben 19:35

So . . . how honest have you been today? HONESTLY?

Anna 19:38

i only decided i was going to BE honest last night! give me
a second

Ben 20:45

Hahaha. I think you've got this, pal. You'll be a truth-teller
extraordinaire by the end of the week, mark my words.

Anna 21:27

thank you, i'll try!

Anna 21:27

gonna tell some truth and tick off challenge two like a PRO

Ben 21:30
Yeeeeeah, she's on a roll. Who KNOWS what you'll do
next! Maybe you'll resign from your position as chief
Broadacre Buddy. Maybe you'll leave Marsha on read.

Oh my god.

Anna 21:32
it's marla!!

Ben 21:33
On READ!

The embarrassment from last night still hasn't hit me, and I'm
wondering if this means it won't. If I think about it properly,
there *is* something horrifying in the fact that Ben knows as
much about me as he now does. If I think about it again, I
realise that really, he knows more than Marla. He knows more
than my dad.

I can't remember the last time I let myself vent like that
without already starting to worry about the repercussions of
it all. But the strange thing is that doing it this time hasn't
left me feeling judged, or regretful. I don't feel vulnerable,
not like I thought I would. Just . . . seen. Sturdier, somehow.

Like it wouldn't be completely impossible for me to achieve something here.

Last Halloween, we were on a train home from the city centre, and an older guy came up to us and started saying stuff to Marla. Nothing too alarming, but it doesn't really have to be *alarming* to be alarming, is what I've learnt. He was looking at us in a way that made me want to scratch off my own skin, and he sat right down opposite Marla and asked if she had a boyfriend, and she said yes, even though she didn't have one back then. She kept looking at the floor when she said it, and he told her that it was a shame, and that she was too pretty for whoever she was seeing, and she did this quiet little giggle that I remember thinking was completely out of character. I knew then that she was scared, because I was too, but something took over and I said, *she's got a boyfriend, we're on our way to meet him, thanks*, in a stern voice I didn't recognise. He looked at me like I'd just kicked him, and said, *I'm not talking to you, I'm talking to her.* And Marla still had this smile on her face like it was fine, although the smile was fixed and empty. I looked at the man and I wondered how he'd ended up like this, why he felt authorised to wander over to girls on trains and steal even a second of their evening. Then I said, *oh my god, read the room*, and I grabbed Marla's clammy hand and took her further down the train, walking through carriage after carriage until my heartbeat had slowed down and I was sure he wasn't following us.

Natalie won't tell restaurants if they get her order wrong. It's happened a couple of times when I've been with her, and she will hiss, *I didn't ask for this with cheese*, but when someone comes over to check on us, she'll say, *mm, lovely, thanks*. This doesn't make any sense to me. It's not like the server will take it personally if you say, *Sorry, no, this order isn't quite right. Would it be OK to send out another one, please?* But Natalie won't do it. She just chews and smiles.

I guess my point is: it's always been easier for me to open up to people I don't know. Challenge them. Cry in front of them. Tell them I think they're wrong. I can do it, sometimes, just like I did with Ben last night, because their opinion of me doesn't really matter long-term.

It's different with the people who are a constant in your life – if you have to see someone every day, you *need* them to like you. I will chew and smile for those closest to me.

That's why I'm scared at the thought of challenge two. *Honesty*. It's not just about the doing – it's about the reaction, the retaliation, the knock-on impact. The fear that when you finally pluck up the courage to tell someone the truth, *your* truth, they'll just come back twice as hard with their own. If there are multiple perspectives battling it out like gladiators, whose wins? Doesn't everyone think they're the one in the right?

I consider texting Ben to ask this, as it feels like the kind of thing he'd have several thoughts on, but I don't. Instead,

I reply to Ryan's message from earlier – something about the art coursework – and wonder where his dad is, right now, at this exact moment. In some Travelodge down the road from Ryan's grandparents' house? Back in Liverpool, working out another plan for the same time next week? My face scrunches up in grim realisation as I picture having to worry about this every day.

We meet in the park on Saturday at Ryan's request, to walk his dog, Chester. I'm unsure of how he's expecting it to go, whether he's invited me for discussion or distraction, but after his revelations in the art classroom, either one feels like something that should probably eclipse my other weekend plans.

It always feels odd to be surrounded by happiness when you're in the midst of something sad. He's a willowy statue waiting on a bench as I approach, and the nearby screams from children and familiar ice-cream jingles feel jarring, almost inconsiderate. Ryan nods, and I smile. It's the tooth-free version I practised in the mirror at Ben's house, polite and artificial.

'All right?' Ryan says, a half-greeting, half-question that doesn't really need a response. Chester looks up at me with big, dark eyes.

I nod, slightly out of breath, and crouch down to stroke Chester's golden head. *Such a good boy. Such a beautiful boy, aren't you?* Chester beams at me.

'How's everything with you?' I ask Ryan from the floor. I genuinely have no idea. He's been quiet again at sixth form this week, making me wonder if he's felt embarrassed since our conversations, overexposed by the information he's shared with me. He hasn't mentioned anything new about his family, and I've been nervous to push it, so any conversation has been stiff. On Tuesday, we talked solely about Natalie's love of reality TV. On Friday, he pointed at the Aragorn stickers on my phone case and asked, 'Who's that man?' I explained animatedly, taking him through a brief explanation of my love for *Lord of the Rings*, and Ryan said, 'Oh. I don't like that sort of thing.'

'All right,' he repeats, except lower this time. He keeps touching his ear, tugging at the bottom of it. The lobe has turned pink and I want to bat his hand away, like Joelle does when Marla's chewing on her nails.

Chester pulls forward, glancing back at both of us as if to say, *well, shall we, then*, and Ryan and I follow his lead.

We walk in silence for a minute or two, Ryan jolting every so often when Chester sees a squirrel or another dog and tries to yank away from his grip. A woman coos, *hello, you*, and I grin loosely in her direction, thanking her when she says how cute our dog is. Ryan doesn't react.

It feels like a good time to check how he's doing. It feels like that's why we're here.

'Has anything changed with your dad and . . . all that stuff?'

All that stuff. God. But I don't want to scare Ryan off, so it's just *stuff* today. Just a casual question on a casual Saturday afternoon, in case he wants to talk. I keep my eyes on the dog in front of us.

'I mean . . . my mum's changed her number now. So, yeah. That's a plus.' He sounds sarcastic. 'He hasn't been back.'

'Oh! So that's good, right? Maybe tha—'

He cuts across me, snapping. 'It doesn't mean he *won't* be back, does it.'

'Right. Sorry.'

Ryan shakes his head and pulls a face: *no, don't be silly.* Then he sighs, ready to elaborate. 'To be honest, I don't think there's any chance he'll properly leave us alone now he knows where we are. That's what we're trying to sort out.'

'OK.' Everything I'm saying sounds hollow. *Right. Yes. OK.* Empty, filler words. 'Does . . . does Miss James or anyone know about this?'

'Yeah, they do. And, like, it is what it is, but . . . we *left*, Anna.' His voice breaks. 'We left Liverpool and we said it was fine but it isn't. I kept telling Vicky it would be all right – even when she was crying about saying goodbye to her friends, I was like, "Birmingham will be better; you'll meet new people and we'll be away from him". And now he's found us. There was no point in any of it.'

He kicks at an empty Diet Coke can in his way. I don't know what to tell him.

'Would he . . . would he hurt you?'

Ryan shakes his head again quickly, without moving his neck. I try to keep my steps very quiet.

'It's mostly the mind stuff. He gets in her head.' He points at his own temple with two fingers, like a gun. 'We tried to leave before – we went to her friend's house – and three days later we were back. He told her all this bullshit about a wake-up call, but as soon as we were with him again he was exactly the same. Worse, probably, 'cause he was so angry she'd left. I can't do that again. I won't.'

We carry on walking for the next few minutes, Ryan talking sporadically and me replying when I can think of something to say that isn't terrible and futile. The conversation isn't easy, but it's helped by the fact that we're side-by-side, eyes and bodies active, dog leash in hand. *We might not have bonded naturally*, I think, *but this is all he has right now. For a couple of Broadacre Buddies, we're managing.* When we go to leave, I give him a hug, gripping him around the shoulders for a second. It feels stilted and self-conscious, as if he's a distant family member I haven't seen in years, but he still looks touched. 'Thanks, Anna.'

Marla 15:32
do u think i should message him

Anna 15:35

i don't know marls – maybe wait a few weeks until you've both had time to think stuff over?

Marla 15:39

i just want to tell him i'm sorry

Marla 15:39

i genuinely think we are supposed to be together anna. there is no one else i could like this much

Marla 16:45

oh my god i just tried to call him and it literally rang twice before he sent me to voicemail. fucking VOICEMAIL

Marla 16:48

answer your phone!!!

Fifteen

'Did you take a look at that *Dada and Surrealism* book in the end? The one for your art coursework?' my dad asks.

We're sitting at the dinner table, surrounded by sketches and tracing paper, and I've got a mouthful of baked beans, which provides me with a few seconds to consider my response. As I swallow, I nod. I'm not lying – I did look at it. I just didn't do anything else.

My dad mistakes my silence for modesty – usually accurate – and smiles. 'You'll be fine, whatever you choose. You're a creative cookie. Always have been.'

He's so wrong this time that I'm not sure how to challenge it. How to say, *no, actually, I don't have any ideas and I used up all my time helping Marla and Ryan, and now I've got nothing to hand in tomorrow.* So I don't. I ask him about a new BBC show he's watching on a Monday night, because I know that's the sort of thing he would want to discuss. It's about a woman who goes missing and how her husband will stop at nothing to find her, but the village they live in is eerie and full of secrets. It sounds vaguely interesting. I tell him I might watch it with him, but I know I probably won't.

'Are we doing anything for Grandad's birthday?' I ask, partly to keep the conversation away from me. The woman on the radio announces that the time is now 6 p.m.

'His birthday? Oh, god, that's soon, isn't it,' he says, throwing his fork down and looking at me with slightly panicked eyes, as if Grandad has sprung this on us.

'It's this weekend.'

'Right. Yep. Saturday?'

God.

'Sunday. Eleventh of October?'

'Eleventh of October! *Yes.* Eleventh of October.'

He grabs a pen from the pile of junk next to him, flails around for a piece of paper, and writes: DAD, SUNDAY in big red letters. I study him while he's doing it. I look at his worried frown and the thin skin beneath his eyes and in my head I shout, *IT SHOULDN'T BE UP TO ME TO REMEMBER THIS! YOU SHOULD KNOW YOUR OWN FATHER'S BIRTHDAY! IT SHOULDN'T BE UP TO ME TO DO* ANY *OF THIS!* In my head, everything spills out and fills up the room around us like a flood.

Maybe now is the time. *Be honest,* I think. *You feel something. For the first time, just say it. Try it.* But then I think of the detail:

the hurt that could fill up his face if my inner shout emerged as words. The busy week he's just had and how he'll be working, again, right after we finish our food, because of the project deadline he's got coming up. The inevitable awkwardness that I know will stalk us for weeks if I address this now.

Nothing comes out of my mouth. I am so angry I could cry.

The sun has well and truly set when I arrive at Malini's house on Tuesday, and as she opens the door she looks to the sky and groans.

'Ugh, *look*. I hate it when it starts to get like this.'

I laugh, shutting out the cold behind me. 'Me too. I'm strictly a spring and summer girl.'

It's true, completely. Everything feels simpler when the day stretches on ahead of you and the night is short.

Malini nods in agreement. 'The only sensible way to be, really. I don't fare well in the winter.'

'My friend Marla loves it,' I tell her, as I peel my coat off and fold it over the banister. 'She starts decorating for Halloween months in advance. She likes the sun as well, but she's just very big on festivities. Christmas and . . . candles and stuff.'

'That's sweet. Although my mum would take one look at her and say, "you're wishing your life away, girly".' Malini smiles. She's putting on lipstick in the hallway mirror, pressing her mouth against a tissue to soak up the excess.

'My mum would say the same,' I murmur, without thinking. Then I do think, and I change the subject to Charlie, quickly, quickly, quickly.

When I hear Ben's key in the lock I leap to attention, ready to rehash the last seven days with him. He dumps his bag by the staircase, kicks off his shoes and gestures at me to follow him down the hallway towards the kitchen, like we don't require the niceties any more. I traipse after him, mug in hand and socks padding on the carpet.

'Tell me straight – has there, or has there not, been any honesty this week?' he asks, selecting a can of Fanta from the fridge and nudging the door closed with his side.

I say, '*bleugh*,' and shrug emphatically, like a grumpy toddler in need of a nap. Ben raises his eyebrows in amusement.

'Well, then. I will take that as a no.'

'Please do.'

I'm enjoying this. Being given permission to veer away from the classic-Anna responses means I can try out some new versions and see how they fit. *One day,* I think, *one day I will show new-Anna to everybody, and they will all just have to deal with it.*

Ben takes a swig of his drink and sighs contentedly. His hair looks different today. Neater, maybe. '*So.* If challenge two hasn't worked out yet, what's gone wrong?'

There's no point in any kind of pretence – not any more – so I tell him about my dad's subpar memory for family birthdays. About the walk with Ryan and my confusion over what being a Broadacre Buddy is supposed to involve. About being pulled along with Marla, again, with no way to ever stop it. Ben's sitting on the countertop now, his legs swinging back and forth, gently thudding on the white kitchen cupboards. As I speak, he nods at appropriate intervals. Then he brings his legs to a halt and arranges them on the surface underneath him instead.

'I've got to ask – why didn't you just tell your dad what you told me? I don't think it's unfair to remind him that his seventeen-year-old daughter *probably* shouldn't be the one in charge of his social calendar.' He sips at the Fanta, offering the can to me like we regularly share drinks.

I shake my head. 'Good question. I thought I might've been overreacting, that it might've been unfair to him. He's got a lot on. Extra work, so . . . I don't know. Sometimes it's easier to just say nothing, isn't it?'

'Definitely, but if you never kick off about stuff that's upset you, how are people supposed to know not to do it again?' asks Ben, matter-of-factly.

He's right. He's so right that I suddenly feel vulnerable, newly aware that – again – all of our conversation has revolved around me and my issues. My flaws. My boundaries. My dad. I flail around for something to serve the attention back with.

'What's *your* dad like?'

It feels like a mistake the second the words leave my mouth. Ben suddenly loses all movement in his face, as if someone's drawn the curtains and shut out all the light.

'My dad's actually dead.'

He says it very calmly, like he's telling me his dad's popped out to buy some cereal, and then studies me with interest as I search for an appropriate response.

'Ben, I'm *so* sorry. I didn't know – I thought . . . I thought he and Malini had divorced and he . . . lived down the road or something.'

Marla's face and elven plait pop into my mind. We're sitting on the science block bench and she asks about my first babysitting evening, and then she says, *I swear this is the friend whose husband walked out a few years ago or something.* That's what Marla told me. That is definitely what Marla told me. I cringe under the weight of this new knowledge, the fact that I never even bothered to check.

'I'm so sorry,' I repeat once more, knowing he must hear this every time he mentions his dad. Why do words never feel good enough when somebody tells you news like that? Why is everything such a puny offering? I wish there was a way you could know exactly what a person wanted to hear at any one time – which combination of letters would help them, and which would make everything ten times worse. I claw on to the kitchen table with one hand, scratching at a peeling bit of wood near the corner.

Ben shrugs. 'It's fine. It was three years ago. Not that that makes it easier, but you don't have to say you're sorry. I can . . . I can talk about him.'

'Yeah, but I didn't even . . . '

I trail off, dejected, and Ben steps in. I get the impression he has to do this every so often and has a small speech prepared as a result. 'He was great. Not a perfect, faultless angel like everyone always wants you to say, but great. He liked AC/DC and cars and he worked really hard. He and my mum met when they were at school. She had me when she was eighteen, *really* young, and everyone said it was the worst idea but . . . ' He gestures to the house we're standing in, looking proud. 'They managed.'

He says all this quite brightly, without the emotion I'd expect from the current topic, but I notice that his eyes are darting around the room, refusing to settle near mine. A fourteen-year-old Ben pops into my mind, next to a baby Charlie and a speechless Malini. It makes me shiver.

'They definitely managed,' I say. 'And your mum is amazing, so I'm guessing your dad would've been, too. Is he the man in the photos on the stairs?'

He smiles with his mouth, but not his eyes. 'Yeah. *Darren*.'

'Darren,' I echo, feeling the word on my tongue. 'You look a bit like him.'

'Really? Everyone always says I'm my mum.'

'You're both. That's the nice thing.'

Ben draws himself up like a zip. 'That *is* nice. However,' he continues, 'we're not talking about my dad. What about yours? Question of the day: why doesn't he just use a calendar or write things down, like everyone else?'

I laugh, a lot louder than I would normally. 'I don't think he'd be so good with that. We used to have one of those family planners in the kitchen, but . . . my mum . . . '

'Oh. She sorted all that stuff?'

'Mm-hmm.'

Ben and I haven't discussed my mum before. Talking about her makes me feel light-headed, like I'm due a nosebleed.

'Where is she?'

I wonder if this is a question he's wanted to ask before but hasn't quite known how to. It was inevitable it would come up, I guess – it's something that always gets discussed, somehow, with everybody, eventually. She always winds up being mentioned. At sixth form: *make sure you show that to your mum.* When I bump into acquaintances of hers who don't know she's gone yet: *how's your mum?* In the shops in March: *these for Mother's Day?* Maybe Ben has the same troubles in June.

'She lives in London.'

I'm not meaning to be obtuse, but this is the only way I can do it. Short, sharp bursts. A few words at once. Otherwise it'll tumble out of me, red and real and dangerous, and I can't let that happen right now.

Ben nods. 'With a new . . . partner?'

'No. With a friend she went to school with. They have a flat in Clapham.'

'Wow. That's—'

'Not a very *mum* thing to do?' I interrupt him, spitting the words harshly.

'Yeah, I mean . . . how did that happen?'

My chest has started to hurt and I pull out a loose hair grip from the side of my head, picking at it with my thumb. 'You know at the start of *The Hobbit* when Gandalf is trying to persuade Bilbo Baggins to go on an adventure with him, and Bilbo says no, because adventures make you late for dinner?'

Ben pauses, and a new expression passes over his face. 'Yes?'

'Well, I guess it was a bit like that, if Bilbo had never changed his mind. Things were bad for a long time. I don't think I really knew they were as bad as they were, but . . . they were. My mum is so different to my dad – she always had all these plans. Like, she wanted to go travelling, and write a play, and find a job in advertising. She wanted more kids, as well – not just me. And my dad . . . isn't like that. He's quite creative too, but he's more traditional with it. He doesn't like adventures. He just wants to do his job and watch TV and go to sleep.'

The light-headed feeling is still there, but I trudge through it.

'I think after a while it just got to her. She did a lot – all of the tidying and the encouraging and the organising – and my dad was just sort of *there* by the side. I used to hear them argue about it sometimes. She'd be like, *how come you still get to* be Paul Campbell, and I have to be everything? I didn't really get what she meant then.'

'Jeez,' says Ben. 'Do you get it now?'

'Yeah, I do. But she still left us. And now she actually *has* a job in advertising, and she lives with some woman I don't even know.' *Saffron.* I met Saffron once, at my mum's birthday party when I was small. She called me Hannah.

Ben frowns. 'That sounds difficult. *So* difficult, but . . . it doesn't sound like she left *you*, though.' He pushes it, telling me the exact opposite of what I wanted to hear from him. 'You can still see her, right? That's a start.'

I pull a face as I shake my head. 'No. I don't even want to. She *did* leave me. I don't owe that woman anything.'

The last sentence makes my heart heave. I picture my mum listening in – a sad, sorry fly on the wall – and I tell her I didn't mean it. *I read all of your messages,* I say, *but I can't speak to you yet.*

Ben's smiling at me sadly, like something new makes sense to him.

'There's that line, "*Not that Belladonna Took ever had any adventures after she became Mrs Bungo Baggins,*"' he says. 'But your mum sounds like she's having a *lot* of adventures now. Isn't that a good thing?'

I know the quote, but I still shake my head.

Ben 21:35

I was just thinking, and you know what? I feel like you did OK this week. Maybe it's not quite worked out how you wanted it to, but at least you knew what you needed to be honest *about*. That's pretty huge in itself. Now all you need to do is take it further. Honesty forthcoming for Anna's dad!

Ben 21:38

Thanks for asking about MY dad, too. I don't really talk about him because sometimes it feels easier not to, but I also think it's somehow harder not to. No idea if that makes any semblance of sense.

Anna 21:49

it makes many semblances of sense and i am very glad it was OK to talk about. i am here for chats like that if you ever need them

Anna 21:49

also . . . thank u for the honesty pep talk. didn't even think of it like that

Ben 21:56

You should! What you're doing is great. Plus, it's all little steps, right? Bilbo had many a setback on his adventure, but he still made it to the Lonely Mountain and lived to tell many tales about the whole thing.

I smile into my hot chocolate. *Little steps.*

Sixteen

Everybody else has a sketchbook full of ideas. I have nothing, other than an urge to pick up my bag and run.

Aisha, an art acquaintance, is sitting slightly further down the table clutching a selection of fruit-themed screen prints. 'They're just my first attempt,' she tells me, waving a hand modestly like they took minutes.

Another girl in the corner has an A1 board with her, one of those thick, black ones that says, *I know what I'm doing.* I try to ignore it.

'Did you manage to think of anything?' asks Ryan, unusually inquisitive. He's been different since our walk at the weekend – more involved, somehow. On Monday, he brought me a fresh bottle of orange juice after I told him I preferred the style with pulp in. I asked about his orange-juice enthusiasm and he said he couldn't explain it – it was just there and always had been. *A citrusy constant,*

I suggested, and he laughed. On Tuesday, after another brief dad update, he sent me a message that said:

> your the one person I can talk to about this.
> Makes me feel better.

I replied with a smiley-face, pretending my shoulders hadn't tensed up from the weight of being his only friend.

He's glancing at the pencil in my hand now. I stop tapping it on the table and shake my head.

'Mrs Gana probably won't be that bothered, though,' I announce breezily, unsure of who I'm trying to convince. 'I've handed in everything else on time, ever, and there's always at least one person who forgets or needs an extension.' I'm not making that up. There *is* always one person who forgets or needs an extension. It's just that this person has never been me.

Ryan does one of those unconvincing, ever-so-slightly patronising smiles that people reserve for when you least need them. It makes me panic.

'What are *you* doing? Which topic did you choose in the end?' I ask him defensively, peering at the edges of his bursting sketchbook. He goes to grab it, placing his pencil case on top of the pages as protection. Then he clears his throat.

'Ordinary to Extraordinary.'

I nod, like I know exactly what he means by that. 'Oh. Sounds like a good one. What kind of thing will you focus on?'

Ryan coughs again, then glances to his left to check no one else is listening in. Aisha and Molly are deep in conversation; he seems satisfied that we won't be disturbed. 'It'll all be to do with music, somehow. Probably sounds cheesy to you, but I kept thinking about it – how you listen to a song or watch a band play and it'll take you from one to the other. Ordinary to extraordinary. Nothing to something. I tried to explain it in my outline, like . . . if I hear the right thing at the right time, I could . . . I dunno. It makes me braver. It makes me feel like a stronger version of myself, you know?'

His arms are still folded across his sketchbook. There's a smudged pen note on his left hand that says MILK.

He's right – it does sound cheesy to me, because it isn't mine. But that doesn't mean I don't hear him, that I don't see where he's coming from in some way.

'Actually, that's kind of how art feels for me,' I tell him. 'I have all these thoughts and all these worries, but as soon as I start drawing, there's suddenly somewhere to put them. I could never be brave enough to just *say* certain stuff, but I could be brave enough to paint it. And then it's as if the painting's saying it on my behalf. You know?'

He nods, face brighter, as though that's exactly what he meant. 'Yeah. It's like . . . if *you* can't shout, you need to find something that can.'

We look around the room at other students' work – charcoal Eiffel Towers and watercolour flowers and acrylic cats. I wonder if they mean anything different underneath. I wonder if anybody in here can shout, or if they've all needed to find something that can take on that job for them, just like we did.

'It's a really good idea. The music thing,' I tell Ryan, and he grins, the first grin of his I've seen in a while.

'Thanks. I'm sure yours'll be a good idea, too. You just need to work out what it actually is.'

As I go to leave at the end of the lesson, Mrs Gana catches my eye and waves. My stomach knots together.

'Anna?'

She waits until everyone else has filed out, taking her time as she washes a handful of brushes at the sink. I lean against a table while I watch her, inhaling the familiar smell of warm water mixed with paint and trying to fill my empty lungs with calmer air. Then she turns back towards me. 'I noticed you didn't hand any planning in today.'

It doesn't sound like an accusation. Just something she's happened to observe.

I give her the spiel I rehearsed in the shower this morning, trying not to blink too much. I'm semi-honest. I tell her what she needs to know: that I'm a tiny bit behind right now, that I've got ideas forming somewhere but just nothing ready to hand in. That I'm sorry. I still want to join the Art Society this term, yes. Very busy. Something-something-yes-definitely-soon, very soon. I can't quite identify the expression on her face, but if I had to hazard a guess I'd opt for 'surprised disappointment'. Something about that makes me feel truly miserable.

'I'm happy to wait for you, Anna – that's not a problem. You can bring me your plan this time next week,' Mrs Gana says, and I try to do a self-deprecating nod that says, *I'm ridiculous, I know. My life won't be a mess for much longer.* She doesn't seem convinced.

My phone vibrates against something solid in my bag – first once, then again three times in a row, like an unruly heartbeat. Mrs Gana's eyes flick over to it, then back again, and it makes me uncomfortable.

She continues. 'This isn't like you, though, is it? You told me you were thinking about art courses for university, so this is the worst time to take your foot off the gas. I understand there's a lot of work to focus on right now, but . . . you've just got to make time for it.'

I make a confident *mm* noise. The bag vibrates again, and the faintest frown lines appear on Mrs Gana's forehead.

'Tell me if you need any help, Anna. You owe it to yourself to see where your art could go. And grades aside, well . . .' Her gaze is a constant, holding me accountable. 'The way I see it is this: if something's important to you, you make time for it.'

'So . . . you didn't hand in your art plan yet. What's the problem?' asks Marla, one hand in a bag of salt and vinegar crisps as we begin the walk home.

Her bluntness makes me feel weaker, like none of my problems will ever matter at all. 'There isn't one, I guess. I just haven't had much time to think about it.'

She offers me a crisp and I take one without thinking, forgetting it's a flavour I don't like. It tastes of metal, almost painful in my mouth.

'There is a very simple solution here: go home this week and get everything done. That's all it is. Literally . . . do the work. You said you have some ideas, right?'

She gives me a similar smile to the one Ryan provided earlier. I return it for fun when she's not looking, flaring my nostrils for emphasis.

'Yeah. I mean, it's fine to do. It's planning for an extended project, and that's fine.' *Fine.* 'But . . . I don't know. The last few weeks have just been pretty intense, that's all.' *Just.*

I'm trying to be honest again and I'm willing her to read between the lines here, like I would. If I had spent every day since my break-up asking my best friend for advice and reassurance and ninety-seven-minute-long phone calls, I would read between the lines. I would say, *shit, Marla, have the last few weeks been intense . . . because of me?* Then she would admit that they had, but she would say it was OK because we love each other a lot and that's what friends are for, and I would say, *even so, I'm sorry. I will calm it down now,* and she would think, *phew.*

But Marla stops chewing and says, 'Everything is intense. Just do your art, babe.'

Seventeen

Ryan 21:10
Hey Anna

Ryan 21:12
do you fancy the cinema this weekend?

The truth is that I don't. What I fancy is spending Friday to Sunday in my room with the door closed, sketching on my bed. Ordering a giant pepperoni pizza on Saturday night and eating it with one hand while I carry on uninterrupted, something dreamy and relaxing playing in the background. My purple light projecting against the walls, making me feel safe, like I live in a little UFO. I fancy waking up on Monday with a fuller sketchbook and a calmer chest, the kind of person Mrs Gana gives a proud smile and an instant A to. I fancy switching off my phone and pretending I didn't see this invitation at all.

I sigh with my entire body. It isn't Ryan's fault – he wants to make friends. He's got to make friends. But sometimes it feels like I'm running so fast and nobody ever stops me to see if I need a rest or a drink or if I even wanted to start running in the first place.

Anna 21:36

sure pal, what about friday night?

Ryan 21:57

yeh Friday night is great. I'll check what's on x

Marla 22:48

just realised this weekend is when me and carl would have gone to london. we were gonna eat at the rainforest cafe AC. THE RAINFOREST CAFE!!!

Anna 23:30

☹ ☹ ☹

Marla 23:33

do you think he'll still go??? what if he's kept the hotel booking and he invites someone else and i have to spend my friday evening eating doritos with the cat while they fall deeply in love in the capital

Anna 23:35
i'm sure he won't go any more! maybe you need a distraction – me and ryan are gonna do odeon on friday night, wanna come?

Marla 23:37
yes oh my god YES. i will even take an evening with ryan over the doritos thing

Marla 23:37
why are u going to the cinema with him???

Anna 23:38
i think he's just lonely? he's got no friends and nothing to do, i still feel bad for him

Marla 23:39
lmao. PITY: the start of all great friendships

'Be honest: do you think I look like a 90s PE teacher?'
    'Only in a good way,' I say, meaning it, but Marla has already

discarded her vintage sports sweatshirt and started to rifle through a nearby drawer. She pulls out an oversized striped T-shirt, holding it up against her in the mirror, then throws it over one shoulder on to the bed, saying, 'oh my *god.*' We've been doing this for almost an hour.

I watch her for a few moments as she paces the room, visibly tense, then perches on the edge of a chair in the corner. She's tearing pieces away from her fingernails again. I never get to see where they end up. I wonder if she has to spit them out when nobody is looking.

Marla's room is still more or less the same as it was when we were eleven. Everything is painted bright yellow (*like a sunflower,* mini-Marla used to tell me proudly) and the bed-sheets are faded blue, soft and loved to near-retirement, with tiny white clouds scattered all over them. Over the last couple of years, one of the four walls has been hijacked and covered in photographs – mostly of Marla and me. My favourite is from Halloween last year. Marla is dressed as a haunted house, her black shift dress embroidered with windows, floating curtains and ghosts. She started work on that outfit in August. I am a last-minute mouse, complete with smudged-eyeliner nose and whiskers. Marla has both arms around me and our faces are pressed close together, grinning and alive.

Things were more fun before Carl, I think. Then I immediately feel terrible.

'What about this?' Marla asks, breaking into my thoughts.

She's wearing a pair of loose tartan trousers, belted at the waist, and a wine-coloured vest top that stops just before her bellybutton starts. I nod enthusiastically but she still picks at the trousers, staring like they might be untrustworthy.

> **Ryan 18:52**
> So good news, my mum has spoken to someone.
> She called up and they helped her. And they think
> she may be able to do more this time, like we might
> be able to stop him coming anywhere near us

> **Anna 18:53**
> oh wow ryan, that's the best news!! will you let
> me know what happens?

> **Ryan 18:53**
> Yeh

> **Ryan 18:57**
> Are you on your way in now? I'm nearly there

Almost 7 p.m.

'Shit – we need to go, Marls. We'll miss the train,' I tell her. She grabs her jacket from the clothes pile on the bed and makes a growling noise that sounds like it came from an animal.

It's impossible to keep up with Marla. She paces ahead of me through the city, her legs double-speed, zipping ahead even though she's tiny. When I catch up, it's because she's stopped at the side of the street outside a newsagent, crouching down to re-roll one of her trouser legs. She looks up and her eyes flash dark.

'Why does this one look *longer* than the other?'

I don't know what to say and the question feels rhetorical, so I just stand there, moving closer to the grimy shop window when an old man cycles past and scowls at me for lurking aimlessly in his way. Marla finally finishes her alterations and emerges from the floor, slightly breathless. She turns towards the shop window and uses it as a makeshift mirror, first tousling her black hair and then stepping backwards to assess everything else.

'OK?' I ask her.

She shrugs softly, crossing her arms as she maintains self-conscious eye contact with the glass. 'I'm just scared I'll see him. And I know I won't really because why would I, what are the chances of that even happening, but I wanted to be prepared and not, like, creeping around with greasy hair or wearing *jogging bottoms*. And then we had to rush but I've never worn these trousers before and I thought they were OK at the time but they actually look ridiculous, and ...'

She trails off.

Marla never looks ridiculous. All we're doing is standing at the side of the road and three girls have already glanced in our direction because she is dressed like somebody you want to know. Her jaw-length bob is *just* messy enough and her checked trousers are resting on beaten-up boots that make her resemble some sort of trained assassin.

'You know what?' I say, grabbing her hand and continuing our walk to the cinema. 'Even if we did see Carl on a jogging bottoms day, you'd still look like a very small supermodel.'

It's true and I want her to hear it, to laugh at the *very small supermodel* comment like she would have done before, to do that cute nose-scrunch she does when she's feeling mischievous. But she doesn't. She does a half-smile, scraped up from the very bottom of her face, and I realise she doesn't believe me at all.

There are small pockets of people outside the Odeon, talking, laughing, shouting, smoking, kissing. One figure is waiting alone, and I can tell it's Ryan even from a distance. His long arms are jutted outwards, elbows pointed as he scrolls on his phone. I speed up my walk. *Ryan!* He glances up, and his face relaxes in recognition. He waves back.

'Jesus,' says Marla under her breath when she reaches me a moment later. 'Is he wearing a *shirt*?'

Ryan does look smarter than usual, and suddenly also confused. He puts his phone in the pocket of a coat I haven't seen before and glances from me to Marla a few times. Then his eyebrows tighten in the middle and he steps towards us, exhaling as he loosens the button nearest his neck.

'All right?'

'Yeah!' I say, 'Yeah. Sorry we're a bit late. The train was delayed, and we had a trouser issue.'

Marla stubs at the floor moodily with the toe of a boot and I feel a prickle of anxiety, like I might have betrayed her by mentioning the trousers. Ryan shrugs.

'Didn't know there was gonna be a *we*, to be honest,' he says, and it hits me that I never remembered to tell him Marla would be joining us. There's never been any vocal declaration that she isn't a fan of Ryan's, but I know he's probably picked up on all of the eyerolls and sighs she hasn't made any effort to hide over the past few weeks. Why did I think this would be OK?

'Sorry,' I hiss quietly as we walk into the cinema foyer. 'I know you and Marla aren't really close. I should have mentioned it – I just thought it'd be nice for us to do something as a group.'

Ryan finally makes eye contact. He's pulling down on his earlobe again, the same way he did when we walked Chester last weekend, and something about him looks pained. 'We'll need to buy another ticket, won't we. Might as well get in the queue.'

The second the film is over, Ryan tells me he needs to leave.

He mutters something about not wanting to miss his bus, standing and striding towards the screen's doors before I have chance to argue. I go to get up too, unsure if he's expecting us to follow him, but by the time I'm holding my coat he's already disappeared.

Marla pulls a scathing face in the direction of the exit and finishes the last of our shared popcorn, legs stretched out in front of her while the crowd disperses. I close my mouth and sit back down, placing the coat carefully on Ryan's empty spot.

Anna 22:28

where did you go?? i'm sorry i forgot to tell you i was bringing marla! i just wanted you guys to get to know each other better

Ryan reads my message as Marla and I step on to the train home, but goes offline instantly afterwards. I start to type another one, a different way of explaining exactly the same thing, then catch myself halfway through and backspace it all. I don't want to assume the worst. What if his phone died? What if something bad happened with his dad this evening? What if he really *did* need to catch that specific bus?

'I just don't get why he'd run off like that,' I tell Marla for the second or third time, as we curl into opposite window seats.

'He's being a damn baby. Next time tell him th—' she starts, then stops. Her whole body goes rigid and her eyes are now dedicated to something that's happening outside the train, metres away from us. I lean forward to see what she's looking at but she holds out her hand to say, *no. Stay.*

Then, as quickly as she froze, Marla relaxes again, crumpling back into her seat as her eyes fill with tears. 'I keep thinking I *see* him,' she says, and her voice gets angrier on *see.* 'Why won't he go away?'

Wordlessly, I glide over to the side she's sitting on, curving one arm around her. There's a group of boys about our age walking up the stairs on the opposite platform, drunkenly shouting into the night. Marla leans into me, resting her head on my right shoulder as the train shunts away from the station, and I bring the other arm up to make a clasp, to clutch her tightly, so full of fierce love for my friend that my own eyes sting.

She sobs into my coat the whole journey home.

Eighteen

Ryan doesn't speak to me at all over the weekend. *No worries!* I keep willing him to type. *You were right – it* was *fun to bring Marla. I just didn't want to miss my bus.* But nothing materialises.

As the rain comes down in sheets on Sunday afternoon I sit in a listless sort of daze with our chat open in my lap, and consider contacting him again. *How's your weekend going,* I could say, *and was everything OK on Friday night?* But it wasn't, and I know it wasn't, so I don't even think that would help. I try to work out what might.

My go-to would be to tell him I'm sorry, again. To soak up all blame like a sponge, no questions asked, knowing that this is a tried-and-tested fast-track back to normality. It might not be honest, but it's all I know.

What *would* be honest? I try to forget the filtered, *see-it-from-someone-else's-perspective* response I would normally try to produce, and instead search for the instant, deep-down,

snap reaction that I had on Friday night and buried away before it had chance to take shape. And honestly? I feel angry. Or if *angry* is too strong, I feel irritated. Vexed. Annoyed with Ryan's complete lack of ability to deal with altered plans. I try to picture the scenario reversed – if Marla had turned up with Aleks, if Ryan had brought a friend from back home – and if there might be anything about it that would rile me. *No.* And I get that Ryan and Marla haven't exactly bonded, that Ryan might feel slightly less comfortable in her presence than in mine, but why would that mean he had to leave without explanation and – worse, in my eyes – ignore a message that made it clear I hadn't intended to upset him?

'Ryan, I think this is a *huge* overreaction,' I say out loud to no one, like it's a dress rehearsal.

When I arrive at art class on Monday, I'm more focused on speaking to Ryan than I am on avoiding Mrs Gana. She shoots me a look that says, *you'd better be working on that coursework plan*, and I send a smile back that I hope replies, *almost done.* Then I take a seat at the table Ryan and I usually opt for, near to Aisha and Molly from the other form. We small-talk for a few minutes as normal, Molly grilling both of us for our views on a boy called Joshua whose messages are lengthy but infrequent. 'I just don't understand what it meeeeeans,' she says, and Aisha and I offer potential explanations I'm not convinced either of us really buy into.

Molly is just beginning to tell us her theory on Joshua's parents' divorce when Ryan walks in. He's wearing headphones that he doesn't bother to take out as he sits down, and when I ask him about his weekend there's an awkward silence, either because he doesn't hear me or because he pretends not to. Molly side-eyes him nervously. I feel my cheeks go red and admit defeat.

As soon as the lesson ends, Ryan slams his sketchbook shut, picks up his bag, and leaves. I don't follow him. I don't try and wave at lunchtime, as he walks straight past with a sandwich that he takes to eat outside. I don't even hang around at the end of the day to see if he might want to talk.

It's for the best, because Marla *does* want to talk.

'Thank *god*,' she says, grabbing my arm as we leave Broadacre. 'Look. Look at this.'

She thrusts her phone towards me so I can assess a screenshot. It's a photo from Instagram, posted by someone called Isabella who has a right-angle jawline and white-blonde hair that looks like she's been growing it since birth. In the image, Isabella is nestled among three other people on a large leather sofa: a grinning boy with bright orange hair, a petite

Black girl wearing Perspex glasses, and – my eyes grow wider with recognition – *Carl*.

'Now. I know the girl with the glasses isn't an issue because she's dating this ginger guy,' says Marla, agitated yet organised. 'I checked.' She looks as if this is news she would like me to write down.

'But that doesn't mean this other girl automatically *is* an issue, though. Who is she?' I ask, using my thumb to point at Isabella's pouting face.

Marla shakes her head at the sky. I get the impression she's already reached a conclusion she's hoping I'll validate soon.

'AC, if your boyfriend broke up with you and then three weeks later he was sitting on a sofa with some Instagram model he'd never even mentioned during your time together, *would you* or *would you not* be a tiny bit worried?'

I resist the snappy urge to suggest there's no need to be worried, because Carl isn't her boyfriend any more. If I wasn't the kind of person who can only tell the truth to an empty bedroom, that's what I'd say. *You can finally relax,* I want to point out. *Please just do it.* We've been waiting to cross the road forever.

'I'm not sure,' I say, as we make a run for it. 'It's not like *Carl* posted the picture. They might not even really know each other. I don't think he would start seeing some random new girl so soon after ending things with you.'

'Well, *I* think you're wrong,' sniffs Marla.

'Can I see again?'

I take the phone from her and zoom in on the screenshot. It looks like they're in some sort of bar or expensive restaurant – there are people in the background wearing shirts, holding drinks, subtly adjusting their hair. *Ginger boy. Glasses girl. Isabella. Carl.* Carl definitely doesn't have his arm round Isabella – their bodies are touching but more due to lack of room than anything else, I'd guess. One hand is in his lap and the other is on the side of the sofa, placed over the leather with confidence. Isabella is sitting with her legs moved to the side and her back slightly arched, like she might have practised this pose at home.

Marla attempts a smirk now, interrupting my unspoken analysis. 'Her posts are all very predictable – just blurry cocktails and *kettlebell* videos. And you can tell half of her selfies were taken on the same day.'

'Oh,' I say. It feels like we're pulling an imaginary person apart, and I hate it. I never know how to respond when Marla gets like this.

'And I don't even think Carl would like her dress sense. He likes girls who wear this stuff.' She sounds hurt, tugging at her favourite leather jacket. 'Not . . . *gym leggings.*'

'Well, then that's good.' There are a few moments of silence. Desperate, I try to create some kind of diversion. 'Marls, I forgot to tell you – I did my art planning. The stuff I was worrying about. I've just got a tiny bit more to finish and then it'll be sorted.'

I've decided that my project will be called Everyday People, the ones that you chew and smile for, because what's more Anna Campbell than that? It was easy to fill pages on Sunday night, to forget about sleep, to rip out illustrations I'd done over the last few weeks and pretend they were something deliberate and exploratory when I glued them into my sketchbook with annotations. There's an artist I follow online called Coco Dávez, whose work makes me feel charged and woefully inadequate at the same time, and I used her as colour inspiration for the next steps, cutting out magazine clippings for some pages and decorating others with neat acrylics. I shoved some Julian Opie in, too, remembering the dog-eared Blur poster my mum used to have up on the kitchen wall. She appeared in my head as I closed the sketchbook, raising her eyebrows at me in the same way Mrs Gana did last week. I knew it was the sort of offering she would call *lacklustre.*

'Told you it'd be fine.' Marla's head is still down, the focus on her phone. '*Look*, she went to California last year. As if I want to see this shit.'

I sigh internally, hurt, then stare at the photo obligingly and make the sort of face I think Marla would find comforting. Isabella is posing underneath an In-N-Out Burger sign on the side of a building, dressed in tiny shorts and a bikini top. You can tell that the sun is moments away from setting – she's squinting behind her sunglasses and her skin is golden, like a painting. She looks good.

'She looks *horrendous*,' Marla snips. 'She looks like every other standard girl who went on an overpriced holiday and got their mum to take slutty pictures of them next to some basic tourist spot. It's embarrassing. Natalie's cousins live in San Francisco and *she* told me that In-N-Out isn't even that big of a deal over there.'

It's strange, because I don't even think Marla buys into what she's saying. She's always wanted to visit California and I know for a fact that she would happily pose by an In-N-Out restaurant, the same way she did when we went to London and took photos outside Buckingham Palace and underneath that famous light-up screen with the Coca-Cola advert on it. She would pull a peace sign, or put both hands flat underneath her chin like an angel, like she does when she wants me to comment on her make-up. She'd probably even wear something fairly similar to what Isabella's got on – just a messier, more Marla-y version of it. But Isabella is a threat, and Marla deals with threats by finding faults in every ounce of their existence.

Before I manage to catch myself, I tell Marla that In-N-Out is probably very overrated, that we would probably just skip it and find somewhere with decent veggie options, probably somewhere near Santa Monica Pier, and she nods approvingly a few times, like, *yes, of course we would.* A pang of guilt, some kind of sorrow, forms a spike in my chest. I don't know why we're doing this. I don't know why I can't just say to Marla,

Isabella being great doesn't mean that you're not. Isabella being great doesn't have any impact on you at all. But it goes deeper than that. It would take more legwork than that, and I don't even know where we'd begin.

Marla continues, identifying several other things that would make Isabella lacking as a girlfriend: her broad shoulders, her tacky sternum tattoo, the fact that she didn't appear to visit Yosemite during her Californian adventure. She looks up afterwards with triumphant eyes, desperate for confirmation.

Honesty.

'She can't change what her shoulders look like.' My voice sounds brittle, as though Marla could reach out and flick me and I'd fall straight over.

'I don't want her to change what her shoulders look like.'

'I know. I'm just saying.'

She crosses her arms, like I've spoiled everything, and swallows, hard. 'Why are you *siding* with her?'

'There aren't any sides,' I say, noticing my own arms begin to shake. 'I just think . . . we don't know her. We don't know her, and she can't help having broad shoulders.'

'She can help being a boyfriend-stealing little bitch, though!' Marla's voice comes out cruelly, all buried anger and caustic sing-song.

People always say that honesty is the best policy, but with Marla it isn't, and I should have known that. She needs bite-sized chunks, little drops of truth-telling mixed with constant reassurance that *she* is the one in the right. The prettiest. The wronged party.

'Let's try and forget about Isabella. You can come back to mine tonight, if you want,' I say. I try to offer her something new, to walk some tightrope between facts and kindness, but she isn't listening. Her hands are deep in her pockets, thoughts multiplying again. There's no hint of blue above us – just thick grey sky, suffocating like when you wake up to snow and the world is suddenly void of colour but there is nothing you can do about it. It makes me want to climb a beanstalk and tear a giant hole in the clouds.

Nineteen

'Here,' says Aleks. 'You'd better be passing those out in the cafeteria, my gal.'

I take the stack of A5 paper from her and read:

RED HAIR? DON'T CARE!!

BLUE CURLS? NICE, GIRL!!

NEW DREADS*? CUTE HEAD!!

PINK 'DO? GO, YOU!!

<u>No</u> hairstyle is 'impractical'.

If you agree that the oppressive hair-related regime at this school has gone on for long enough and that the way you choose to wear your hair* should not be deemed in any way reflective of your ability or eagerness to learn, then please join me by signing the online petition at **change.org/broadacrehair**.

Aleksandra Kowalska

*PARTICULARLY for our Black and POC students, Mr Decker. I urge you to respond to Year 11 student Tiwa Bankole's campaign RE Black hair as a matter of urgency.

'I will do my best,' I say, smiling at her and meaning it. She winks at me, making an exaggerated *click* noise with her mouth, and wanders towards the playing field with her hood up and a cardboard box of print-outs tucked under one arm. I put my own pile into my bag, leaving a few rolled up in my cardigan pocket for easy distribution, and head in the direction of the shortest lunch queue.

There's a small snake of people waiting for food, and at its tail is Oliver, a shy boy from my history class who I haven't spoken to properly in years. He spots me and nods, his dark hair glistening with rain specks from outside.

'Hey, Anna.' There's a water droplet on his glasses, now smudging as he wipes them. I want to reach out and rub at it with my sleeve, the way my mum used to do when I had something on my face.

Oliver nods again, this time at my pocket, and says, 'Are you helping Aleks with the No More Impractical Hair Detentions campaign?'

I laugh, impressed he's already heard of it. 'Kind of. I'm on leafleting duty but I feel like an imposter because I've never actually *had* a detention for my hair' – I point at my long, reddy-brown mane – 'or any detention, actually. So I'm here to support.'

His eyes are sincere. 'Me, neither. I've signed Tiwa's petition, obviously, and I'll look at Aleks', too. It's a different thing entirely, but I don't see why she shouldn't have blue hair if she wants it.' Then he squints. 'I can see *you* going full red or something. That could work.'

It makes me smile, mostly because I can't see it at all. 'Thanks.' He returns the expression and we move with the queue-line, edging nearer to the serving area.

'Jesus. At it again?' says a loud voice to my left. I whirl around towards it, startled, and scan the immediate area. *Ryan*. He's standing next to a large A3 version of Aleks' poster, hands in his pockets, glowering in my direction.

Oliver visibly recoils, then shifts his attention to the pizza slices a few feet away from us, as if he's suddenly forgotten he even knows me. My head starts to throb with confusion, thoughts clambering like tiny ants in a swarm. At *what* again?

'What d'you mean?' I say after a few seconds, but Ryan's already turned away. He strides towards the exit of the cafeteria, throwing his empty juice bottle into an en-route recycling bin with sarcastic enthusiasm. I stay rooted to the spot.

'What do you *mean*?' I repeat to his back, volume raised, knowing he won't hear me. A few people at the tables nearby have started to stare in my direction, sensing an unease and enjoying the first sniff of potential drama. Nobody says anything. Oliver keeps his head down.

'Sorry. I need to go,' I say, and Oliver coughs, very quietly. Pushing past the people who've gathered in the queue next to us, I slam my tray back down on top of the clean pile and set off in pursuit. Down the three stairs, into the entrance hall, out the main door – and there he is, propped up against the wall by the music block.

'Ryan!' I can hear my heartbeat thudding in my ears, fast and angry. 'What's *wrong*?' My voice sounds odd: strained and pleading.

Ryan looks at the floor. 'Don't ask about it. Just go back inside and leave me alone.'

I don't. I move closer to him, stepping forward so we're face to face. It feels daring.

'Why did you just say that? *At it again?* At what? Is this because of Friday still?'

He doesn't say anything. He just sighs once more, sullen and lethargic, refusing to meet my eye. I try to set up and maintain some sort of glare but the silence knocks me and I feel too exposed. I wind up staring at Ryan's left shoulder instead.

'Friday was a bad idea,' he says, finally, and I glance back up.

'Why was it a bad idea?' I push. 'Was it Marla? Or did you need to talk to me about your dad or something? Because that's all you needed t—'

Ryan cuts across me, his voice suddenly harsher, and it shocks me so much I step backwards into a girl holding a cone of chips.

'It's got nothing to do with that!' There's another pause while he runs one hand through his hair desperately. 'Just . . . stop messing people around, Anna.'

I want to ask him to repeat himself, because I'm pretty sure he just told me to stop messing people around. As if that's something I do. As if that's a regular Anna Campbell activity. The girl with the chips has continued on her way but is looking back at us now with bright, unabashed interest. Ryan is biting down on his lower jaw, clenching together so the sides of his face jut out slightly. Then he crosses his arms, like he's suddenly self-conscious. I try to pick out some words from the jumble my brain has provided me with.

'I don't see how I messed you around. I'm . . . I'm sorry

I changed the plans, I genuinely am, Ryan, but I don't understand why it's bothered you this much. I said I was sorry. I said th—'

'I don't need you to say *sorry!*' He jolts, his hands moving away from his body angrily. 'I need you to stop treating me like this when you clearly don't mean it. Checking up on me! Helping me! Asking about my fucking dad! You know more about me than most people back home but when I ask you out, you show up with *a friend*?'

A strange feeling floods through me, a heat that starts in my ears and dives down towards my toes like a wave. *Asked me out?* I try to remember the words Ryan used in his text, the words I used in response, but the ones I can recall are all innocent: *Cinema. Sure! Pal. Great. I'll check what's on.* The silence sits in the air on top of us as I blink and Ryan stares straight on, his face and his breath hard, waiting. *I want to stop time,* I think. *I want to freeze the world and run away.*

'Ryan . . . that wasn't what I thought about . . . any of this,' I stammer. 'You're my friend. I really thought we were friends.'

His eyes are fiery. 'Then why did you keep making it more? We hung out all the time. You messaged me all the time. Are you telling me I'm a liar?'

I feel a shudder of irritation across my shoulder blades, sharp enough. *I didn't message you all the time. You messaged me all the time, and I replied because I was supposed to be looking after you.*

He interrupts my thoughts, mocking them. 'Oh, let me walk your dog with you, Ryan! Bring me orange juice, Ryan! Tell me about your family, Ryan!'

My face burns with humiliation. I'll have to tell everyone that I got it wrong. Marla will roll her eyes and say she *warned* me it was a waste of time, and they'll all laugh at me for being so nice, for not knowing these strange, unspoken boy-rules that they're so familiar with. *If she's kind to you, she likes you. If she agrees to accompany you to a Hollywood blockbuster on a Friday night, you're good to go.* Maybe Ryan was expecting something mediocre from me – neglected messages, aloof responses to his news – because that's what usually happens?

'Look,' I tell him shakily. 'Mr Bains asked me to be around for you. You heard him. And I said yes, because I'm . . . bad at saying no, and you looked like you needed someone. And you *did* need someone. I didn't want you to be alone.'

I wish so badly for Ryan to nod at this new clarity and say, *now I get it! Thanks for explaining, Anna.* But he doesn't. Disgust is slowly creeping across his face.

'So you were just . . . doing a job? That's all this is?'

He's deliberately twisting it.

'No!' I say. 'I mean – I was doing a job when I said yes. But we get on OK, and you told me about your dad, and . . . ' I trail off, pathetic. 'I thought I was your friend.'

'Well, you didn't act like it,' spits Ryan. 'So . . . '

He takes out his phone from a pocket and begins to scroll.

The cruelty of it feels like a fresh sting.

'Ryan, I never meant for ...' I begin, but his eyes stay glazed over and the words get lost in my mouth.

Twenty

There's a tiny crumb balancing precariously on Ben's lower lip. He senses my eyes flick towards it and wipes at his mouth with a sleeve. Mortified, I look away.

'Does anyone want a prawn cracker?' he says. 'And by anyone, I mean you.'

He's standing in the living room, arm cradling a plastic bag full of them. I'm on the sofa still, the triangle of my folded legs covered by a chocolate-coloured blanket Malini usually drapes over the reading chair by the window. I keep tucking and re-tucking it around me, pulling the edges in tightly like a neat hotel bedsheet.

I shake my head. 'I'm fine.'

'Band practice, however, was *not* fine. Jimmy never buys replacement guitar strings and Ayaan had a sore throat, so we gave up and got a takeaway instead. But you know what? That's the beauty of having minimal talent and no fanbase whatsoever. No one to disappoint if you decide to take the week off.'

'Yep.' I shove my sketchbook into my bag.

He squints at me, smiling. 'Do you have places to be, people to see?'

'What?'

'You seem rushed. Or maybe I'm talking too much. I'm sorry. I will hush so you can leave the Brennan residence and go and live your actual life.'

'No. It's OK.' I can feel my insides squirming, *hating* this evening's forced coldness, but I don't know what else to do. It's like being back in Niccolo's with Marla, deliberately neglecting my thank yous, pretending to be somebody else, somebody unapproachable. 'I'm fine.'

Ben cocks his head to one side. 'Yeah – you said you were fine a few seconds ago, but I'll be honest – you are giving off very non-fine vibes. *Incredibly* non-fine.' A laugh breaks out of me, letting the side down, and Ben beams. 'There she is!'

'I *am* fine,' I say, catching myself and deliberately looking at the floor. 'I just . . . I had a bad day. I'm still processing.'

'Oh. D'you want to talk about it?' He sits softly down next to me, leaving space between us. I appreciate the gesture.

I shrug. 'Thanks, but there's nothing to even say. It's more of the same – Anna's too nice.'

That's all it is. That's all it ever is – Anna being too nice, doing too much, laughing too hard, smiling too wide. Never managing to hit an acceptable amount. Always tipping the balance slightly and fucking it up.

Ben doesn't say anything. He just waits. So I wait, too, for a minute. I enjoy the stillness, and then I dredge everything up. I spill my guts like I did last time.

When I'm done, Ben sighs, deeply. It's something completely new, a reaction I've never seen from him before. 'Well, we definitely know how Ryan feels. How do *you* feel?'

I wonder how to answer the question. It's like digging deep into my brain with a spade, trying to get down to the real stuff, the ugly emotions I've kept buried on purpose in the past. 'I feel . . . well, I feel embarrassed. But I also feel angry?' My voice goes up at the end, one of those American TV-girl inflections my mum used to tut at. I catch it. 'Yeah. I feel angry.'

Ben snaps another prawn cracker into his mouth, then says, 'I'm not surprised, mate. I would be absolutely livid.'

'You would?'

'Of course I would. Ryan sounds like he's got a lot to deal with, and I really feel for him on that, but . . . I don't know. Thinking a girl being kind to you is some sort of romantic invitation? Feels very 1950s to me.'

'That's what *I* thought!' I say triumphantly. 'And then insulting her when you realise it's *not* anything romantic, instead of just apologising for the misunderstanding! I was going back over all the things I'd supposedly done to make him think I liked him. Asked about family. Texted back. Stuff that I would do for lots of people. I didn't treat him any differently. I thought he was a friend – maybe not a close one, but . . . you know? It was working OK.'

'Is this why you were quiet earlier?' asks Ben. I hear my phone buzz on the table, but for once I'm too engrossed to care what it has to say.

'Yeah. I wasn't trying to be rude – I just felt ridiculous. Like, is this how I'm coming across to everyone?' I shudder at the thought of what I'm about to ask next. 'When . . . when I text you, are you there, like . . . thinking what Ryan's thinking? When we hang out, do you . . . do you think it's because I'm . . . *interested*?'

He shakes his head with conviction. 'Never. You're my friend – I think you are interest*ing*, not interest*ed*. And honestly . . . I don't even think this is about you. I don't know Ryan, but I know Anna, and she's kind, and she's generous. If someone chooses to take that differently to the way it's intended, surely that's more about them?'

That's more about them. I exhale gently. 'I think I'll have a prawn cracker now.'

'I knew you wanted one, really.'

Ben holds out the bag once more and I take a cracker, cradling the delicate shape between my thumb and forefinger before crunching into it.

He grins at me as I chew.

Malini's home late tonight – 'out with a *man!*' Ben says, with raised eyebrows – so we stay talking, only pausing to fetch cake slices from the kitchen when Ben decides he's in need of more food. The light is low and soothing, and something is processed in my mind as we sit. It comes out instantly.

'Oh my god. I think challenge two might be complete.'

He nods at me proudly, like he isn't surprised at all, and I stumble over myself to explain things as they occur to me.

'It is! It's . . . it's *done!* I would never have been honest about something like this in the past – I would have just pretended everything was fine. Or I would've stopped coming here at all, in case you were another Ryan. I would have blamed myself. But today I didn't. I got through it.' The thought floors me. 'This is big.'

'How does it feel?'

It feels *good.* It's not like I've conquered some metaphorical mountain. It doesn't suddenly seem like everything's clicked into place, like I can start my new life as the assertive Anna I was always supposed to be. But maybe that's OK. Maybe honesty is quieter than that. Maybe it's just about coming out with the truth, even if your truth isn't quite the same as someone else's. Is that what happened with Marla yesterday, without me even realising it?

There's a small spark of pride in my chest and I give Ben a nervous smile, unsure of how I'm supposed to celebrate this evening's news. He offers me his water glass and I clink my own against it.

'Cheers to you. What's challenge three?' he asks. He's sitting with his back against the sofa now, elbows rested comfortably.

My phone buzzes twice in my hand.

Marla 21:17

do u think this whole time he just wanted some gym girl who owns a mug that says SWOLEMATES and only eats broccoli

Marla 21:17

ugh. let's do something fun this weekend pls. movie night at mine??

I skim over the text quickly, sigh, and re-lock the screen, my focus on Ben once more. 'No.'

'No challenge three?'

Cackling, I correct him. 'Challenge three is about *saying* no. I feel like . . . if I've managed to be honest, this needs to come next. It's on another level.'

There isn't anything easy about it. The word is barely in my vocabulary – it feels novel, almost frightening, to say, as though uttering it without anything else wrapped around for protection could cause an earthquake; an off-the-richter-scale scene of destruction.

Later that evening, I write the word NO into the niceness notebook, eyes fixed on the familiar green pen. It delivers a spiked N and a poised, defiant O.

> No, I don't want to do that.
> No, I can't make it this evening.
> No, that's not OK for me.

I stare at the page, breathless. Soon I might be able to say these things out loud, and not just write them.

Twenty-One

A familiar nausea hits me when I see she's been in touch.

Mum 07:03
Thinking of you, sweetheart. Wishing you a good day.
Mum xx

Ten words. Two kisses. She always used to send one, a singular x, a uniform sign-off for everybody. Maybe she feels like she owes me the addition these days.

I read the text so many times that the word *wishing* starts to look strange, as if there's a possibility she made it up this morning. Then I press hard on the delete button, ready to pretend nothing ever arrived here at all. My phone asks if I'm sure, and I say yes, in my head and out loud. The message disappears, off to join the others in a virtual graveyard.

Things from my mum always pop up when I'm least

expecting them – when I check my lock screen lazily from the sofa at Marla's house, when I'm bleary-eyed first thing in the morning – and they floor me for at least a day. It feels like they come from a ghost. A sensible person would try not to disturb a ghost. If you were brave, you would ask it to leave you alone.

The worst part is that sometimes I want to make some kind of contact. Sometimes I wish I could speak to her like I used to – call her up and say, *hi, I just wanted to ask you something.* She would always sit there thoughtfully while I was talking, occasionally nodding and smiling, but she would never interrupt. I think my mum is the only person who ever did that for me.

Marla listens but she doesn't always *listen*-listen. Occasionally she will butt in to say, *look at that girl's dress* or, *oh, a cat!* and then she will quickly say, *sorry, sorry, carry on,* and I will, a little less certainly, until she does it again. Aleks and Natalie always try to solve things, even though some things can't really be solved and seem to exist purely so you can worry about them. My dad just clams up. But my mum would let me speak until I had exhausted myself, knowing that was normally all she needed to do.

When I told Ben about my mum, everything that came out felt like anger. I said I didn't see her, that I wouldn't text her back, that she left us. I was telling the truth. I haven't seen or spoken to my mum since the seventeenth of January. And considering I used to see and speak to her every day, that's kind of messed up.

Do you not think it's odd, Marla said once when we were half-asleep in her bedroom on a rainy Sunday afternoon, *that you are nice to everybody except for her?* I told her I *was* nice to my mum, very nice, until she came into my bedroom on New Year's Eve and told me she would be leaving for London soon because that was the life she'd decided to live. When people ask about her, I always miss out the part where she asked me if I wanted to go, too. *It's your choice, Anna,* she'd said. *I need to do what feels right for me now, and you must do whatever feels right for you.* I told her that nothing in this situation would be right. How could moving a hundred and twenty miles away to live with your mother and a new flatmate called Saffron feel like the best course of action? How could it be any better to remain in your childhood home with a father you've never really got to know properly?

I miss out some other parts when I tell the story. Like how I cried so hard on the day she moved out that I was sick and it felt like a chunk of my soul got flushed down the toilet with everything else. How on the day of my GCSE art exam she'd written me a note before she went to work that said, *Anna is an ARTIST. I have so much faith in you, sweetheart x* and I saved it to keep in my bedside table with my other important things. It still lives there, but I don't look at it because I don't want to remember the good of it all. I want to remember the bad at the end, because strangely, that hurts less.

What would my mum have to say about Ryan? I can guess. She wouldn't Marla-railroad things, demanding to know why I befriended someone I clearly have nothing in common with and accusing me of excessive niceness. She would probably ask gentler, more inquisitive questions, like, *do you really* want *to have Ryan back in your life?* Or, *why do you think you felt so drawn to help him?* And I would probably end up crying and say that I didn't feel drawn to help him, not even slightly, and that I only agreed to it because the thought of turning down a request like that is too much for me to handle and then things went too far. I think my mum would understand that.

When she and my dad were together, I never paid much attention to what they were like as people – not as parents, or a couple, but literal human beings, separate from anyone else. Afterwards, it was all I really thought about. How my mum's friend Beth would call her up and say, *can you take the kids on Sunday again, Gem?* and my mum would say yes, that was fine, but then she would put the phone down and sigh very softly. How she would always stay late at work, even though she hated work, because *who else is going to do all that?* My mum would understand almost everything with Ryan, I think, so long as I explained. *She* never knew how to say no, either.

She appears in my head now, a version of her that I can remember. She sits at the foot of my bed in that dark purple dress my dad used to love – I can see her, right down to the way she moves her hands to explain herself, all flowing gestures, silver rings, long fingers fluttering like butterflies. It makes me realise she still exists, that she's a real person, out there somewhere still having these kinds of conversations with other real people who aren't me.

The imaginary-mum smiles, ready to talk. I don't smile back. I try to ignore the new sadness in my stomach, the fact that she left me here to deal with this on my own, but the more I fight it, the more it twists and contorts into something else, a rising anger.

Why didn't you teach me to stand up for myself? I rush straight in, not bothering with any re-introduction. *Why didn't you show me? All I do is say yes to everything, and it doesn't make me happy. It wears me out. And now I have to be the one to teach myself how to do it differently.*

She stays in her original spot, calm despite my outburst, exactly how she used to be. *But remember, you are nice, Anna. You're kind and that's what we love about you – that's what everyone loves about you. There's nothing wrong with saying yes to new experiences. There's nothing wrong with wanting to help.*

There is, though! I explode. *You can't do everything. You can't help everyone. You can't always be the perfect girl who doesn't mind – sometimes you have to say no. Why am I the first person in this family who seems to realise that?*

There's a new expression on her face now – a kind of thoughtful amusement, like I've said something she's somehow way ahead of. I can tell, even in this made-up world. She tucks her long hair behind her ears and I see a glimpse of the earrings I bought her for Christmas last year, the little hoops with the crescent moons hanging underneath them.

I open my mouth to push further, to demand an explanation – but as I do, my phone vibrates against the bedside table. And then she's vanished, as quickly as she came.

Marla 07:22

oh my god . . . isabella is going to the birthday presence
gig tomorrow night

I sigh. *It doesn't matter what Isabella is doing,* I wish I could tell Marla. *It has never mattered what Isabella is doing.*

Anna 07:24

you're not going though, are you? so it's fine ☺

Marla 07:25

no but carl loves birthday presence, we'd said we might
book tickets ages ago. i bet if she's going then he's going

Anna 07:25

maybe, but i don't think it's a good idea to stress too hard
marls. there's nothing we can do about it

There's nothing we can do about any of this. Why do we even know which local concerts Isabella is planning to attend?

Marla 07:25
just checked and tickets are available still

Marla 07:26
tomorrow night. will u come with me

Marla 07:26
please anna

Marla 07:26
i just wanna see

No, I think. I type the word out and stare at it for a second before spooking myself. Delete.

Anna 07:26
i know but it's my grandad's birthday meal tomorrow night, we're all going out for food

We only do this – only meet up properly as a family like this – once or twice a year. *Say no, Anna. Tell Marla you won't budge. You're getting somewhere with all this now, and it isn't so scary when you've already started.*

Marla 07:27

could you see him another time? i promise i would NOT
ask if it wasn't important. i don't wanna go alone to this

Why is she planning to go at all? Why can't she just bow out
with dignity and say, *have a nice life, Carl*?

Anna 07:32

i can't come ☹ i haven't seen my grandad for ages
and i said i'd go

Marla 07:33

please???? i'm not gonna do anything weird i'm literally
just gonna see if they're together so i can move on with
my life!!!

Within seconds I've already played out the evening in my
head like a film: Marla nodding graciously at whatever outcome
we've encountered at the gig, telling me how much calmer she
feels now she knows for sure. Us leaving early, going to get
barbecue vegan burgers on the way back to the train and sitting
in contented silence as we chew. Marla deleting Carl's number
from her phone, smiling through watery eyes and saying,
*well, at least we have an answer! Now I never have to think about
it again . . .*

The thought of Marla moving on with her life is enough to

prod me into action. If this is the turning point – the gigantic signal from the universe that she'll need in order to go forward without Carl – then I need to help get her there. I *want* to help her get there, so we can finally leave Carl behind.

She's *typing*... still, hounding me for a decision.

Anna 07:35
i'll see him another time, it's OK. you can book the tickets

Marla 07:35
i love u AC. thank you thank you thank you xxxxxxxxx

Twenty-Two

I'm zipping up a pair of jeans on Saturday night when my dad knocks gently on my door. I tell him to come in. He's wearing a shirt, the checked one he always returns to when we need to do anything that involves family members. It's supposed to be non-iron, but there are enough creases in it to make me think otherwise.

'Are you sure you don't want to join us?'

I swear his eyes look hurt. I've been expecting it, and I brace myself to disappoint him again.

'No, I'm OK, thanks.' I'm trying to sound flippant, to seem sure of myself. 'We really like this band, and I've already told Grandad I'll see him another day. He's fine with it. Will you take him his present tonight?'

My attention flits from one thing to another while I wait for my dad's response. I pick up a pair of socks from the pile of freshly washed clothes on the bed and sit down to put them on, deliberately taking more time than normal. Slowly. Methodically, like when parents put clothes on to toddlers.

Maybe, I tell myself, *maybe this is what it feels like to say no. I might not have got to that point yet with Marla, but this is still some kind of progress with my dad.* I always show up for Grandad's birthday. I was the one who *remembered* Grandad's birthday. I bought the gift. I wrote the card, and left a blank space on the left-hand side for *Paul xx*, even though *Paul xx* had no involvement in any of this and doesn't deserve the prime signing spot. So maybe this *is* what it feels like to say no. Maybe this is Anna Campbell completing challenge three ahead of schedule.

My dad nods and does a very small smile. It reminds me of the one Marla manages to muster when she's not doing so well. 'Of course I will.' He pauses, and I can tell he's gearing himself up to say something else. 'Grandad'll be sad not to have you there.'

My chest jolts. *This isn't right. This isn't doing what you want or saying no to look after yourself. It's just bailing on your original plan because Marla came up with another.* The thought makes me flinch with guilt, because I've messed up again, I've messed up *again* and it's far too late to do things differently now.

'I know Grandad'll be sad,' I snap. 'But it's *one* birthday. You wouldn't see me kicking up this much of a fuss if someone couldn't make it to mine.'

He blinks at me. 'No one's kicking up a fuss, Anna. I just said you'll be missed, that's all.'

The doorbell rings and we both know it's Marla. My dad sighs, mumbles something about needing to leave anyway. I follow him downstairs with the Grandad-gift-bag in one hand, a black one with gold HAPPY BIRTHDAY lettering that's been passed back and forth about thirty times since it was put into Campbell family circulation. He takes it from me and greets Marla, just a touch less warmly than usual. She doesn't pick up on it.

'Have fun, Paul!'

My dad pulls the door closed after him and leaves Marla lingering in the hall while I put my shoes on, tucking and untucking her hair behind her ears as she gawks at the mirror, mouth open. She smells like perfume and alcohol, like something sweet.

It's not too late to go and see Grandad, a little voice tells me. *You could run after your dad, jump in the car with him now. Marla could even come with you.* I ignore the voice and stand up to leave.

'Ready?' says Marla, like we're going into battle.

I wish so badly that she didn't want to do this.

'Ready.'

The man checking tickets at the venue entrance tells Marla she looks like some actress we've never heard of, and even though it's unprofessional and gross she still giggles like it's the best news she's ever heard.

'Google her – I promise she's gorgeous,' says the man, scratching his neck. 'And so are you. Both of you.' I narrow my eyes at him.

'*Dave*,' says his colleague, looking agitated. 'Where's the sound guy?' Dave nods at a door to the left of the main entrance. She grunts and heads towards it.

'Thanks, Dave,' says Marla, her eyes sparkling. Dave tells us to have a good night and Marla saunters towards the stairs, fluffing her hair up, happy to be watched. She's wearing heeled Mary Janes that her feet don't seem to have made peace with.

It's still early but there's someone on the stage messing around with cables and people have already started to pay attention to that part of the room, a low buzz emerging from the groups dotted around the auditorium. The cable man acts like none of us are looking and carries on. There's a cluster of fourteen year olds gathering behind the barriers in front of him, desperate to secure the best views.

Marla sniffs. Her mood has changed again.

'Is it lame to turn up for the support?' she asks. I know she's only bothered because of who she's expecting to be here. The venue is filling up but the crowds are still sparse, and it dawns on me that if Carl or Isabella – or both of them – are here now, it'll be hard for us to melt into the atmosphere unnoticed.

I still shake my head. I love the support acts. Marla knows I love the support acts. It reminds of me watching the trailers at the cinema – *here's some stuff you will also like, and even if you don't, well, you've paid for it now, so you might as well enjoy yourself.*

But I don't think Marla *is* enjoying herself. Her head bobs from place to place as we watch the first band, her attention solely on the crowd and the people in it. One girl with bright yellow hair and winged eyeliner throws us a glare as Marla cranes round to get a good look in front of her. When the support band packs away after their set, Marla grabs on to my hand and says, 'toilets?' I nod. She keeps hold, her fingers wrapped around mine, and leads the way to the women's bathrooms.

'This is fun, right?' I shout over the music. I sound like an eager mum. 'Even if they're here, it'll be OK. We'll get to see the band. We'll still have fun.'

I'm trying to keep things positive, to keep Marla distracted, but the fact that I've said the word 'fun' twice suggests that maybe we won't have much of it at all. Marla's underwhelmed facial expression seems to echo this suspicion. She pushes on a scuffed door marked LADIES, kicking it gently with her shoe as it bounces back towards us, and we move from the dark, husky box of the venue into the harshly lit bathrooms, where girls are peering into mirrors as they wash their hands.

'I like your dress,' I say to one of them as she checks the edges of her lipstick. She turns around, surprised, and I point at the striped pinafore she's wearing. Her face relaxes.

'Thanks!' she says breathlessly. 'I found it in a charity shop. I've literally never been one of those people who can find things in charity shops – you know, when someone says, "oh, I just found it in a charity shop", and you think, "how, because I *never* find things in a charity shop?". It was like that. Except one day I *did* find something in a charity shop. And it was this.'

She stops suddenly, as if she's just hearing herself and she's not sure if she should continue. I laugh and tell her it was a solid find, and she beams at me.

'You ready, doll?'

A voice appears from behind us, and striped pinafore girl – Doll? – nods at it, bright-faced. She turns to walk back out of the bathroom towards the bar, and as the owner of the voice follows and glides past me, I glance in that direction. The girl grins politely, flipping a sheet of long blonde hair from one side of her head to the other, and my brain stops for a moment while it registers her face.

Isabella.

Marla, emerging from a cubicle, stops dead in her tracks like a musical statues champion. I watch her in slow motion as she desperately scans for in-person flaws while Isabella floats from the bathroom, blissfully unaware of any kind of assessment taking place. Isabella catches the door behind Doll and uses her side to thrust it open again, an old Fall Out Boy song seeping in through the gap before it seals shut behind her. Moments later, a group of girls with identical facial piercings burst in, raucous and drunk. One of them screams when the door hits the wall and bounces back towards them. I stare at the chips in the tile, well-established from where the same thing has happened before, and wait for Marla to move.

She doesn't, for a few seconds, and I can't tell what she's planning. My chest starts to ache again.

'Marls, I think maybe we should leave,' I say quietly. 'It doesn't feel like a good idea to be here any more.'

Marla shuts her eyes for a second, scrunches them up like two paper balls, then breathes out sharply as she reopens them. Striding forward, she grabs my hand again and lurches in the same direction as Isabella, forceful and wobbly at the same time. I can feel the heat coming from her palm. It makes my own hand sticky.

'Don't you think we should leave?' I repeat, more urgently this time. Everything feels dangerous.

'No,' says Marla, as the bathroom door swings behind us. 'I think we should go and see what trustworthy Carl is up to.'

I've never seen Marla properly lose it, apart from the plate-smashing incident. There aren't any plates nearby, I don't think, but there are glasses and people and Isabella and probably Carl and I don't have a clue how this is going to go. I wish Aleks was here. This is when you need an Aleks – to say, *this won't solve anything and you're being stupid, so walk outside, now.* Those words would never come out of my mouth, and if they did no one would listen to them, because no one takes orders from a doormat. I wish I was like Aleks. I wish I was like Natalie, some perfect mixture of kind and powerful. I wish I was like Marla, able to commandeer another person's evening just because I felt like it. She continues on her way, tailing Isabella stubbornly.

Everything has suddenly started to fill up in anticipation of the main act. To the right of the bar there's an array of battered sofas and armchairs that have been claimed as usual, and when Isabella and Doll reach them they head straight for a small group in the corner. Marla stops awkwardly, mindful even in her rage that we shouldn't get much closer, and drags me in the direction of a wide pillar nearby. It's covered in old concert posters and grubby-looking band stickers we can use as camouflage as we watch. Doll takes a plastic beer pint from the outstretched hand of a bespectacled girl I recognise from Marla's Instagram screenshot, and I lip-read as she says, *thanks*. The girl is sitting next to a tall, sturdy-looking silhouette that I know instantly is Carl, and Marla must register him at the same time because I hear her gasp like she's been winded.

Isabella – still oblivious to the two girls watching her ten metres away – pulls a pretend-grumpy face at the lack of available seating, putting one hand on a hip and pouting slightly in Carl's direction. He leans forward into the light, smiling at her half-heartedly, and she's talking to him now, her face animated and confident. Carl shrugs like he's not sure what to say in response to whatever she's asked him, and

Isabella wrinkles her nose audaciously before taking a seat on his outstretched legs and grabbing Doll's beer to sip. She raises an eyebrow at Doll as she does so and Doll smiles gently at her, the smile of a girl who's shared too many of her own pints.

Marla makes a muffled noise. I feel around for her hand in the gloom but she's chewing at a nail, so I grab her elbow instead and we take refuge behind the pillar.

'Well, that's it, then!' Marla cries, clapping her hands together and putting on a fake-earnest voice. There are tears forming in her eyes. 'That is that. Carl has moved on!'

'Marls. You don't know tha—'

She cuts in. 'No, I do know that! And it's funny, really, because he was always so *sad* that I didn't trust him. He always said everything was fine; there were no other girls waiting around to swoop in and steal him! Not even Isabella, who everyone *loved* telling me I was crazy to be worried about! And here she is! Isn't that great?'

She looks like she wants to hit something. A manic teardrop runs down her face, bringing black make-up along with it.

'Glad I didn't worry,' she says loudly to no one, as she turns on her heel and stalks in the direction of the exit. 'So glad I didn't worry.'

I flail for a second, then let her go, and as I emerge from our pillar hideout I aim a covert stare at Carl, who seems to have zoned in blankly on Isabella's back while the conversation continues around him. He glances up listlessly, sensing my gaze, and our eyes meet. Carl immediately stiffens in his chair, focus shifted to who might be with me. He *knows* who might be with me. Isabella turns around and tries to brush something from Carl's face, Doll watching on loyally, and he bats her away. His eyes are on the exit, and I can tell by his expression that he's seen a small, black-haired figure racing up the stairwell towards the main doors. He swallows. Blinks. He doesn't look moved-on to me.

Twenty-Three

My aunt tags me in a Facebook status on Sunday morning.

> **Denise Grant**
> 14m
>
> Such a lovely evening to celebrate Dad's
> birthday. Good food, good company, what
> more could you want!! **Ewan Campbell**
> **Paul Campbell Alan Grant Lara Grant**
> **Ellie Louise Grant Dan Harborne.**
> Missed you **Anna Campbell** xx

There's an image to accompany it: a blurry photo of everyone around a large circular table. I can see a cake sitting proudly in the middle, one of the layered ones my cousin Ellie makes, with hundreds and thousands sprinkled on top. Grandad is clutching the string of a large helium balloon that declares him a BIRTHDAY BOY, his smile so wide that his eyes have disappeared. I spot one empty chair. My chair. They've used it for coats.

'How was last night?' I ask my dad when I venture downstairs, busying myself with the toaster so it seems more of an off-the-cuff question.

'We enjoyed it,' he says, without looking up. It seems a strange response to give, like he's using the *we* specifically to emphasise my lack of involvement. I walk to the fridge and grab the butter, trying to assess his tone retrospectively.

'Did Grandad like the book we bought him?' He's definitely unhappy with me. I can tell by the way he won't meet my eyes, the false dedication to whatever it is he's working on at his laptop. 'Dad?'

He snaps out of it then. 'Sorry. Loved it. Good choice. Look, I've got a lot to get done before the meeting tomorrow.'

I picture all of them gathered at the table in the restaurant, trying to work out why Anna has opted to skip this rare event in favour of some concert she didn't even mention until yesterday. *She's changed*, my dad says, *and not in a good way*.

'Where's Ryan?' asks Natalie, grimacing at a sad-looking sandwich as I sit down opposite her on Monday. 'He hasn't sat with us in ages.'

Aleks makes a loud noise in agreement. Her hair has turned a pale purple over the weekend and she looks like a My Little Pony I had when I was five. 'I saw him in the common room earlier but he just blanked me. Is that Broadacre Buddy thing just . . . done now? He could at least say hi.'

I haven't mentioned the discussion from last week to them. I haven't known how to broach it. *Ryan won't be hanging around with us any more, because he thought I liked him but I didn't, so now he pretends we never knew each other at all. Back to normal at lunch.*

Marla is quiet once more today, scrolling through her phone like she can't even hear what's going on. She's been distant since Joelle picked us up from the station on Saturday evening, going from manic, jabbered speech on the train journey home to a noiseless husk of a thing in the passenger seat of the car. She must have slept badly, or not at all, because she sent a flurry of messages in the early hours of Sunday morning, all capital letters and question marks. I responded as soon as I woke up, but she'd passed out by then. The walk to sixth form this morning felt flat.

And it's not just Marla who's creating a distance. The awkwardness with my dad – the meaning I'm interpreting from our interactions after my last-minute rejection at the weekend – has left me irritated with Marla, as if she knew this would happen all along but kept on insisting anyway, with no consideration of anyone but herself. I think back to what she said, all of the forced spiel about wanting to move on with her life, and I know in my gut that none of it is going to happen.

I should just tell them the truth about Ryan.

'It's not a big deal,' I say. 'But we ended up having an awkward conversation on Tuesday and . . . we haven't spoken since. I don't think he'll be around much any more.'

All three of them instantly stop what they're doing. Natalie abandons the depressing sandwich and even Marla locks her phone, placing it back down on the table next to her and sweeping an offending crumb on to the floor.

'What happened?' says Natalie, and Marla and Aleks look at me as if to ask the same thing. I glance around to make sure Ryan isn't in earshot somewhere, waiting to contradict my side of things.

'Remember when Marla and I went to the cinema with him?' I ask, and they nod. 'Well, I forgot to tell him Marla was coming, and when we showed up he was really annoyed. I think he . . . I think he thought it was, like, a *date*.' I sigh. *Honesty*. 'He definitely thought it was a date.'

My ears feel warm. Saying this out loud feels arrogant somehow, like I'm throwing out examples of how great I am.

Aleks breaks the silence first, snorting. 'Oh my god. Yeah, just a casual date with the girl who's been ordered to show you how to get to maths class. 'Cause she'd definitely be interested.'

I relax, pleased to hear she's not taking it seriously.

'Wow. What did he say when you told him you didn't like him?' asks Natalie, her eyes shining with interest. I wonder if this is like a plot from one of her books.

'He was embarrassed, I guess. And angry. Really angry. He kept trying to say that I'd been leading him on, but I tried to explain that I was just doing what I'd been asked to do. Like, I was trying to make sure he was OK in his first few weeks here. And there was that stuff with his dad that I was worried about. You were, too, Nats. I didn't *mean* anything by it.' I'm embarrassed as I explain myself, unsure of how this defence will be received. I can feel Marla looking at me but I keep my eyes away from her, afraid she'll use this as a *told-you-so* opportunity.

'The curse of the Campbell,' says Aleks knowingly. 'Too good for your *own* good.'

She means it kindly, but I flinch anyway. 'Maybe.'

'Hasn't that ever happened to you, Aleks?' asks Natalie. 'Has no one ever taken it the wrong way?'

'No. Never. If I like someone, they know about it. If I don't . . . well, they know about that, too.'

We laugh, because she's definitely right. Aleks leaves very little ambiguity for anyone.

'Huh. It's happened to me,' says Natalie, her face contemplative. 'More than once. When Oliver Dunn's cat died, I asked him if he was OK a couple of times and he thought . . . you know. And Aleks, remember when I was talking to Jake for a few weeks over the summer? He was just asking for Netflix recommendations, complaining about his job, very boring, very un-flirty. I even went out of my way to call him *buddy*, just so he knew where we stood. Then when I told him I'd been on a date with Tal, he went all weird. And now he doesn't speak to me.'

I nod, validated. 'It's exactly like that.' It feels comforting to know it isn't just me who's experienced this, that it isn't just me who speaks in a language boys can misconstrue. 'Ryan was so *resentful*. That was the worst part – like, the idea of being friends with me was just a waste of his time. It wasn't worth anything to him unless it . . . went somewhere.'

Natalie frowns. 'So strange. What girls view as normal, everyday kindness, boys seem to view as something completely above and beyond. Not all of them, obviously. But I remember reading this article somewhere that said a lot of straight men aren't *used* to having in-depth, emotion-sharing conversations with anyone other than their girlfriend or their partner or whatever. So as soon as a girl asks how they are or goes out of her way to check up on them, they automatically associate it with romantic interest. They can't even help it. It's just . . . how the world raises them to think.'

Aleks groans. 'The patriarchy, ladies and gentlemen. What a dream for us all.'

Malini 17:35

Hi Anna! Thank you for being so great with the babysitting recently, I appreciate it. Just to say I won't need you this week – I've got a rubbish cold so I'm not going to French class tomorrow. See you next week though. Merci!
Malini xx

Anna 19:13

no worries! feel better soon and see you next week xx

Ben 23:56

No Anna's Anti-Nice Challenge catch-up tomorrow, then. Want to fill me in on your progress another time? Coffee on Thurs or Fri?

Ben 23:56

P.S. If you say no, you will have succeeded at challenge three. I'll congratulate you. But I'll also be sad.

Ben 23:57

P.P.S. THIS IS NOT A DATE; IT IS A DISCUSSION (OVER COFFEE). Just wanted to make that as clear as possible.

Anna 08:10

hahaha oh my god

Anna 08:10

but yes!! no idea what's going on and in desperate need of cake from dukes. what about 5ish on thurs?

Twenty-Four

Ben's waiting outside Dukes when I arrive on Thursday. He waves at me dorkily and I do the same back, already starting to pull off my hat.

'Hi.'

'*Hi.*'

We find a table near the window and Ben puts his coat over one of the chairs to claim it. 'I've been thinking about this cake ever since you brought it up,' he says. 'If they don't have the lemon drizzle available today, I will riot.'

I laugh as we join the queue, and he mimes picking up an invisible chair and smashing it. He's wearing his giant grey sweatshirt today, the one that says TOUCHÉ AMORÉ, and when he rubs his hands together – 'Let's go, Anna Campbell!' – I take him in with the rest of my surroundings. The café is dimly lit and cosy, and his nose is still glowing pink from the cold. I wonder if he would get on with my friends.

The thought is interrupted by a barista. '*So.* What can I get you?'

'Your biggest slice of lemon drizzle, please,' says Ben, and the barista laughs.

'Everyone's after the lemon drizzle today! I'll see what I can do.'

They continue talking, leaving me with a welcome minute to select my own choice. *Red velvet,* I think, *or toffee. Maybe toffee.* Ben pays for his cake slice and hot chocolate, taking a wooden block marked 12 and ambling back towards our table.

'Excuse me, do you have any flapjacks left?' says a saccharine voice to my side. A middle-aged woman has appeared next to me, fresh from the street outside and dressed in a beige trench coat. The barista nods, grinning, and the woman relaxes. 'Great. I'll take two. Oh, and an Earl Grey.' She turns to give a thumbs-up to a man seated at the table nearest the door.

'Sure. Just give me a minute – I need to serve this customer first,' the barista says, pointing in my direction as she glides over to the coffee machine.

The trench-coat woman glances at me with surprise, as if I've been invisible for the last few seconds. 'Oh. She doesn't mind, do you, love?'

I falter for a moment, feeling the barista's eyes on me while she works. 'Uh—'

The correct answer is 'yes', says a voice in my head, lightning-speed. '*Yes, I do mind.*' *You don't want this woman to push in front of you. She got here after you. So what gives her the right?*

The woman taps her fingernails on the counter-top, impatient.

I know, I tell the voice, *but we're only talking about waiting an extra few seconds for a slice of cake. It's not a big deal.*

If it's not a big deal, she won't mind being the one who waits the extra few seconds. You were here first.

That's true. I was here first. But—

Look, says the voice, *you have two choices. Pretend this is fine, even though it isn't. Or tell the truth and risk upsetting someone. What are you going to do?*

Tell the truth. I'm going to tell the truth.

'I . . . I do mind, actually,' I tell her, and the words feel sticky in my mouth. 'I'll be done in a second.' I attempt a smile after I finish speaking, to show I'm one of the good guys, just a nice girl learning to stick up for herself.

'Right. Well, if we're going to make a big song and dance about it!' the trench-coat-woman says. Her voice has turned sour and she makes a real show of picking up her umbrella and handbag, sighing as she moves four paces to the right.

'Now, which cake did you want, lovely?' asks the barista. She winks at me with kind eyes that seem to be trying to say something without using words.

'Toffee, please. And . . . and a banana smoothie,' I say. 'Thank you.' The trench-coat-woman groans, like we live in a world where banana smoothies take days to make. I swipe my debit card and walk back to the table with shaky hands.

'Everything OK?' Ben asks as I sit.

I pull off my coat and fold it over the back of my chair, dazed. 'I think so. I just told someone that they couldn't push in front of me in the queue. That lady over there. The one buying flapjacks.'

'What? Who?' He swivels round to assess the coffee shop counter. 'Oh, I see her. She looks *furious*.'

The thought is terrifying. 'Does she?'

'Yeah.' He sounds impressed. 'Good work, mate.'

I try to breathe carefully. I try to remind myself that this woman is a stranger, someone I will probably never see again for the rest of my life. It doesn't matter if she's angry at me.

'See, this is what I hate,' I say. 'Knowing that someone's upset because of something I did. It makes me want to backtrack. Like, I know she pushed in, but what if she genuinely didn't see me? What if she just made a mistake, Ben? Sometimes people make mistakes.'

'Yeah,' says Ben, with a mouthful of lemon drizzle. 'They do. But sometimes they push in front of you so they can get their flapjack quicker.' I screw my mouth up to one side dejectedly and he continues, swallowing. 'I think it's OK to speak up when that sort of thing happens. You weren't rude, right? You just told her you were in the queue first, which you were. She can deal with that however she wants.'

I mull over what he's saying, because at face value it makes sense. When you phrase it like that, it all becomes very uncomplicated – just a back-and-forth between two people, a statement of fact, no need for any dramatics. Yet here I am, endlessly worrying about this stuff. Concocting these stupid challenges, made up of things that other people don't seem to find challenging at all. Setting boundaries, being honest, saying no – why is it so easy for everyone who isn't me? Why don't they struggle like I do?

'What's *your* version of this?' I ask Ben, gesturing to the counter with my thumb. He stops slurping his hot chocolate and makes a questioning noise, like he doesn't understand what I mean. 'The *nice* thing. I mean, this is what I'm working on. What are you working on? What do you worry about?'

He scratches his head, pushing the dark hair to one side and frowning. I can't tell if it's because he can't identify his own deep-rooted personal struggle or because he's working out whether or not to tell me about it.

Eventually he says, 'I think in some ways, I'm kind of ... the opposite of you, actually. So maybe that's it.'

'What d'you mean?'

'Like, you're worried that your thing is phone calls and joining societies and being too nice and giving too much. And I guess I'm scared that I'm the reverse of that. I have my family. I have the band, and the guys in the band. A couple of others. Kat. And Amrit. I have my weird babysitter friend' – I stick my middle finger up as I sip my smoothie – 'and ... well, that's it, really. That's all I'll dedicate my energy to.'

'And you feel like that's a bad thing?'

He's wiggling his leg under the table. I try to ignore it. 'No. Not always. After my dad died it was a very conscious thing, because I realised that what you think will happen isn't always what *does* happen, and I kept seeing so many people wasting their time on stuff they didn't get anything from.' He pauses. 'Like, when I was in Year 10 there was this kid called Elliot who I'd been trying to bond with since the dawn of time. He was really into wrestling, and I'd always try to watch it so I knew what he was talking about, even though it was shown really late so my mum would obviously get weird about it. And then I'd walk in on a Tuesday morning or whatever, half-asleep, throwing out these Seth Rollins facts, and ... I dunno. It wasn't that I didn't enjoy it – it was cool. But I didn't enjoy it anywhere near as much as Elliot, and I only really watched any of it so he'd like me.'

'*Did* he like you?' I ask, staring at him over the top of my glass.

'No. And that's what I'm saying. He wasn't mean to me or anything. He just ... didn't care that much, and for some reason that made me try harder. But it was a waste of my time. And, like, my dad was really into cars and making things, really hands-on, so I kept trying to do that stuff, and ... ' He trails off. 'My point is: a lot of people do that. They pretend to like things they don't like and they laugh at jokes they don't find funny and they go out for burgers with friends they don't really care about. And I'm not up for that any more. Inner circle. That's it.'

'I think that sounds good. It's brave.'

'Ehh,' says Ben. 'But it's not very growthful, is it. Being this way keeps everything very small. I don't really give new people a chance, because I'm already sorted. I don't want to throw time away on stuff I don't like, so I just don't bother trying it out.'

Both sides of this argument make sense to me. I think about whether there could be some sort of middle ground, some way to protect yourself and your inner circle while still remembering to say yes to the things that sound good. I also think about how Ben just told me he doesn't give new people a chance.

'*I* was new,' I remind him, trying hard to sound nonchalant. 'Why did I make the cut?'

I expect Ben to laugh, but he doesn't. Instead he stirs the dregs of his drink with one of those long metal spoons and peers out the window at a man walking past with a large cardboard box. 'You didn't, really.' He looks almost guilty, like I'm expecting to hear something he won't be able to tell me. 'The first time I met you – and no offence, obviously – you sort of . . . you sort of gave off this smiley, everything-is-wonderful vibe. I think it's just your go-to with people you don't know, maybe?' *Ha.* 'And I thought you seemed nice, really nice, but it felt like we'd be completely different, so I didn't think anything about being friends with you. But then when I met you again, you seemed distracted. There was clearly all this other stuff going on and you kept seeming angry, like you had something inside of you that was knocking really hard to be let out.

I dunno. When I saw that, it made me relax around you.'

'Wow,' I say. 'So you liked grumpy-Anna?'

'Everybody would, if they met her,' says Ben simply. 'Actually, I guess some people wouldn't. No one's universal. Who cares? I think it's good to see all of the sides of someone, and that's what made me want to be your friend.'

'The bad stuff made you want to be my friend?' This is such a brutal surprise to me that I feel my eyes water in gratitude. I pat at one of them with a napkin, glad that Ben has returned his attention to the slab of lemon cake.

'It's not bad stuff, though, is it?' He looks up, smiling at me gently. 'It's just normal. Saying that something's annoying, or asking everyone to leave you alone for a bit, or finally admitting that you love Taylor Swift and don't actually have any interest in Marla's punk playlists.' I let out a bark of laughter, and a man nearby jumps. 'You can't control what people think of you. The people who like you will like you no matter what. The people who don't . . . well, I don't think they're worth trying to convince in the first place. You shouldn't have to act with any of us, Anna. You're important, too.'

You're important, too. It feels like there's a little glow forming inside me, a soothing light just above my stomach that sees me and knows me and thinks I'm OK. Ben slurps the last drops of his drink and gets up to use the bathroom, leaving me alone with a busy head. I fish my phone out of a coat pocket and see five missed calls from Marla. Another one comes through as

I'm staring, and I picture Marla on the other end, forever *the main one*, entitled and expectant. What makes her any different from the woman in the queue? When's the last time she did anything to show me I'm important, too – that I'm not just the doormat she can wipe her muddy feet on whenever she decides to?

'No,' I whisper, swiping the red button defiantly. Marla's name disappears from the screen, and it makes my stomach somersault. 'No.'

Twenty-Five

The sun knows I'm celebrating. When I wake up on Friday morning it streams through the curtains, a timely offer of support from the elements, and I stretch out contentedly, happy to have them on board. Ben's sent me something funny and Tolkien-themed – I reply hurriedly before reminding him that I rejected some calls last night and spent the evening painting instead, like someone who's got her life together and completed challenge three. He responds straight away with a tick emoji. I grin, then go to look through all the other things I didn't read last night.

When I reach Marla's messages – all of the follow-ups to her ignored phone calls – my shoulders instantly ache. I skim through each of them, tight knots forming on both sides of my neck.

Marla 17:23
where are u babe

Marla 18:05

just called. are you around??

Marla 18:09

could really use a chat. this isabella stuff is still Not Fun

Marla 19:34

stop ignoring my caaaaaaalls!! love u

Marla 23:20

have i upset you

Marla 23:26

i can literally see you were online an hour ago what the
fuck anna ☹

Anna 07:07

you haven't upset me at all! i was out with ben last
night and then i had a load of art to do – it's just been
really busy

Anna 07:09

see you at 8 ☺

She'll be here in less than an hour and she won't be OK.
Why did I think she would be? Why did I try to convince myself

that Marla would take her rejection like a champ and decide to go do some piano practice instead? I was so proud of myself for saying no, for testing this new routine, I naïvely assumed she would be happy to fall into it with me.

Marla does show up at 8 a.m., like normal, but she doesn't ring the doorbell. Instead, she perches on the stone wall outside the front door. I see her through the frosted glass, legs swinging slowly, and I grab the handle.

'Marls?'

She peers over at me, and her eyes look different today. 'Hi. Come on, then.'

We set off, with more of a gap between us than usual. I do up the zip on my coat and my hair gets stuck in it because I'm rushing. I yank the zip back down. A few strands rip out of my head and stay trapped in the tiny metal teeth, so I pick them out and set them free. They float away. I wonder how far they will travel, whether a bird will use them for its nest.

Marla hasn't said a word since we started walking and the silence is making me nervous. 'Sorry I wasn't around last night,' I murmur, already repulsed with myself for backtracking after feeling so positive an hour ago. 'I was with B—'

Marla interrupts. 'With Ben. Yeah, you said.' She takes a big breath in and sighs deeply. The sigh is so loud that not addressing it would be weird, and that bothers me. I can't work out what the biggest issue is for her – if she's more annoyed that I wasn't available or that I was with Ben.

'I do have other friends, you know,' I say. I'm trying to joke, to do a Natalie and make someone laugh while also making my point, so this clumsiness can disappear, but in my anxious state I'm not sure how it comes across.

She laughs, but in a mocking way, a sneery giggle. 'Oh, well, I'm sorry. Next time, just let me know you're unavailable and I'll leave you and your boyfriend to it.'

What? I turn and look at her, but her eyes are fixed firmly ahead.

'He's not my boyfriend,' I say, because he isn't. A Year 12 girl gives me an uneasy smile as she overtakes us and I'm embarrassed by how juvenile what she heard must have sounded.

Marla ignores me, so I try again. 'He's my friend. You know he's my friend. We went for coffee together because there wasn't any babysitting this week, and it was just a busier night than usual. It was just ... busy ... '

I trail off uncomfortably the second I realise I'm forgetting to be honest again. Not about Ben, but about the reason for declining Marla's calls. *Just busy. Nothing to do with you. Never anything to do with you, Marls.* She doesn't look convinced, and I hate how I'm defending myself, how quick I've been to reassure her that there's nobody else in my life who could ever take precedence. *Your boyfriend has dominated our discussions for months,* I want to point out, *but the concept of me having my own is too much for you?*

'You can be busy and still pick up the phone – it's not hard to reply to a message. Are you genuinely telling me you were out *all* evening?' She sounds desperate, clingy, and it makes me embarrassed for her. Maybe this is what Carl couldn't deal with any more. 'I guess Ben-time is too important.'

'This doesn't have anything to do with Ben,' I tell her. 'I like hanging out with him, same way I like hanging out with you. He's a friend. We just talk a lot, sometimes, so . . . I don't know. He's been helping me with stuff.'

Marla's dark eyebrows have practically fused in the middle. She frowns at me with suspicion. 'What *stuff*?'

'Like . . . life stuff.' This is almost humiliating. It sounds like Ben's running a therapy retreat in the middle of a lakeside forest. 'I told him a while ago that I was trying to work on a few things – things I was struggling with – and he just sort of . . . ended up helping me.'

She does the same abrasive laugh from earlier, the one she does when she thinks I'm being ridiculous. '*Wow.*' I've never heard anyone pronounce their Ws so clearly.

I shrug, hoping it looks faintly aggressive. 'What?'

'I just think it's funny,' she says, and when I try to predict what might be funny my chest lurches so much I feel weak. 'That you've only known this kid for ten seconds and you're already letting him dictate your life. That's hilarious. That's really classic-Anna.'

Classic-Anna? A switch is flipped, a door is unlocked, and I don't even try to hold myself back.

'No,' I tell her. 'No, it's actually not. You don't know me as well as you think you do. I'm not here to be a doormat, and I don't think it's unfair to need a few hours' break after months of helping you constantly. Months, Marls! Why am I not entitled to one day off from your *neediness*?'

'Asking your friends for help isn't *needy*!' she says fiercely. 'All you had to do was pick up the phone, or just text me and be like, "sorry Marla! I'm out! Speak to you soon! Hope you're all right!" It's not difficult.'

It's my turn to laugh now. The ache in my chest has morphed into a fire.

'Yeah, maybe!' I reply, my voice stuffed with sarcasm. 'Or maybe you could have just *called someone else* last night? Texted Nats? Walked three metres to the kitchen and spoken to your mum? Maybe you could have dumped on somebody else, just *one time*, instead of it being me again.'

She starts to say something, to tell me why I'm wrong, but I interrupt, refusing to let her.

'It makes no sense, Marls!' We've stopped walking now, we're standing outside some house and the people on the driveway next door are pretending not to look at us. 'You can't bitch at me in Niccolo's for being too nice and then have a go at me when I try to change that. Pick a stance.'

She rolls her eyes like I'm crazy. 'Jesus Christ.'

'*What?*'

'Those are two completely different things! The stuff with Ryan was ridiculous – you didn't even like him. He wasn't a friend. *I'm* a friend, and last night I needed you. I told you I was upset about Isabella and you ignored me for hours.'

'But you're *always* upset about Isabella!' I spit, outraged she can't see things the way I do. The frustration of the last few weeks is egging me on, reminding me of all the times I've put Marla first and myself second. 'Do you not think I'm sick of looking at her Instagram and hearing about her squats videos and going to gigs so we can stalk her? How does trying to put an end to that somehow make me a bad person?'

She's breathing heavily and little strands of fringe are sticking to her forehead. I look at them while I work out what I might say next.

'I'm nice,' I offer. It comes out sharp, angry, and I enjoy the feeling. 'That is what I'm like. And I'm sick of it. So I'm trying to stop.'

'*Nice,*' she says, another spluttered laugh coming out with the word. 'No. You just have a weird obsession with coming across as perfect to people who don't care about you. Who gives a single shit about helping some new kid settle in just so you don't have to say no to Mr Bains? That's not *nice.* That's pathetic.'

'I know it's pathetic, but that's just how I am!' I say, throwing my arms in the air theatrically. 'I'm nice! OK?'

'Ohh, Anna Campbell, the nicest girl,' says Marla in a fake baby voice. 'You're my friend, and I don't want nice. I want real. I want generous, I want fucking *raging* on my behalf when it's required. Nice is a nothing – it's just sitting on the fence so you never have to upset anybody.'

Suddenly I'm transported back to Dukes – I'm there with Ben, feeling the light in my stomach as he reminds me to be me. Is that what Marla's trying to say too, in her own, blunt, Marla-y way? My thoughts squirm as I try to make sense of it all. If Marla wants me to be real, if she's so sick of nice-girl-Anna, why won't she ever let me put her away?

'Well, it's interesting,' I say. 'Because I've upset you today and you can't deal with it.'

Marla *uggghs* in exasperation, and I push further. It feels like every problem I've ever had, every annoyance I've ever sat on to keep the peace, is finally floating to the surface of something murky. 'I just needed one evening to myself, where I didn't have to text you, or speak to you on the phone, or hear about Carl, or cheer you up, and you couldn't cope. It's exhausting. I don't think you even *want* a friend. You didn't want a boyfriend. You want someone with no life who just exists to make yours better.'

She makes a gasping noise, and for the first time since we started this conversation she looks truly hurt. But then her face hardens again. 'Well, it would've been great if you'd told me you felt this way.'

Then she turns and walks back in the direction we came from, kicking orange leaves from the path in front of her.

Twenty-Six

Marla doesn't show up to sixth form. She isn't there on Monday, either. I wait at home until 8:12 a.m. and then leave, keeping my head down as I pass the house we argued in front of last week. There's no one outside, just a fresh carpet of fiery leaves like the ones we stood on three days ago, and I'm grateful for it. Each time a red car drives past me I look up, searching for her in a vehicle that could be Joelle's but never is.

Ben 08:18
Um – seeing as you've now morphed into a
no-saying, boundary-setting, call-rejecting
Anna Campbell . . . does this mean you
need to set a challenge four?

His eagerness – the pride in his words – sets something off in me that feels like guilt. I swipe the message away, then reach for the niceness notebook in my bag and carry on walking with it open in one hand, reading through all of my stupid scrawlings from the last few weeks.

> I was honest with Marla (I think) about Isabella. It didn't go well.

> I don't know why, but I find it easy to tell Ben the truth.

> Ryan won't speak to me. Now Marla won't speak to me, either.

How do you know if any of this is worthwhile? There's always a loss there. For every positive there's a negative, for every act of bravery there is always something left behind, decimated. You can push it, but there is always someone pushing back.

'D'you know what's up with Marls?' asks Natalie absent-mindedly, as she flicks through a magazine someone's left behind on a common room table. Aleks glances up as she hears Marla's name.

I keep wondering what kind of excuse Marla will have provided Joelle in order to stay home. Will she have made something up – some ailment that's hard to disprove, like an earache or a painful stomach? Blamed it on me? Blamed it on *Carl*? I'm not even sure if Joelle knows about their break-up. Marla doesn't seem to like talking about those sorts of things with her. There aren't many people who *do* know about their break-up, I've realised. The photos of them as a couple are still sitting at the top of her Instagram grid, ready to mark an invisible territory on her behalf. Mementos from their relationship – a birthday card, a stone from Brighton beach, a Happy Meal toy – haven't moved from their dust-outlined homes on her desk.

'I'm guessing it's Carl-related again,' says Natalie, with just a hint of a sigh. She's reading an article titled 'The Dark Side of Fashion: Your Looks in a Landfill'. 'It normally is.'

Aleks raises her brows as if to say, *duh,* and the two of them lock eyes, like this is a conversation they've delved into several times recently and feel very similarly about. Despite my own anger with Marla, I still feel a pull to defend her while she isn't here. But what am I supposed to say? *Well, on this occasion it's actually because I shouted at her on the way to sixth form last week and she ran away crying.*

'No, no, I don't think it's Carl,' I tell them weakly, but Aleks stops me.

'It will be. Like Nats said, it's a given. I know she's your best friend, Anna, but *god*, that girl is hard to deal with sometimes. And over the last few weeks she's got even worse.'

Natalie winces at me, like, *sorry, that isn't how I would have phrased it, but yes, more or less.*

'What?' I say, faltering even more. I've sensed that Marla's moping has had a knock-on effect on the four of us – sometimes killing the mood, occasionally monopolising the conversation – but not to this degree. 'What do you mean?'

Aleks waves her hands around flamboyantly, trying to work out how to word things. 'I don't know. The . . . the Carl stuff. Spending random lunchtimes blanking us all because she's too preoccupied with whatever drama she's worried about that week. *Disappearing* like this and not even bothering to tell us where she is. Natalie messaged her earlier and just got ignored. It's draining.'

All of a sudden, a part of my world-view caves in on itself. *Draining. Drama.* The Marla I assume everyone else always sees – the confident, candid, oil-painting Marla who does whatever she wants – disappears from sight, replaced with the version I thought she reserved mostly for me. Anxious. Selfish. Afraid.

'But Marla's the fun one,' I say, like she's a product I'm trying to sell to a weary buyer. 'I thought you all thought she was the fun one.'

Aleks and Natalie exchange another look, and I can tell they're not quite sure what I mean.

I'm not quite sure what I mean, either.

Twenty-Seven

I'm holding a drawing of a girl with big eyes and brown hair that reaches her toes. Underneath it is the word CHARLIE, all wiggly letters and blue crayon.

'Is this ... *me*?'

Malini nods, smiling. 'Yes. Charlie asked me to give it to you next time you babysat. And I have been instructed to tell you that there is a football next to you because he would like you to play a game with him sometime.' She reaches for the kettle next to her and pours steaming water into two mugs. 'D'you want the teabag leaving in?'

'Please,' I say. 'And tell Charlie that I don't have any football knowledge whatsoever, but I'll see what I can do ...'

She laughs. 'Neither do we. We are *not* a sporty family now, and I think he's running out of options. Oh! I had a text from Ben, by the way. The journey to Berlin was fine. He'll be back on Friday night.'

I don't share that I had a text from Ben, too, because I don't know if he tells her about things like Dukes or that we speak as often as we do. Instead I say, 'great!' and try to look very interested in a story she tells me about her own sixth form trip to Berlin twenty years ago, instead of letting my brain travel to Marla and niceness and everything else.

'How are things going for you?' Malini asks, taking a sip of steaming mint tea. I can't tell if she's referring to sixth form or life in general. I attempt a clumsy slurp of my own drink and it burns my lips.

'Oh! Fine, thanks,' I offer. It seems like she's expecting me to expand on this, and I panic for a second because I'm not sure how to. 'Excited for half-term, I guess. I feel like I need a break.' *Excited for half-term, I guess.* Because I am a six year old, and not even an interesting one.

'Is everything starting to get on top of you?' Malini looks at me sympathetically. I think she means work. She probably means work. She has no idea about Marla, about her showing back up to sixth form today with an absent expression and even less fingernail than before.

Is everything starting to get on top of me? I imagine grey, faceless creatures clambering over a sad Anna Campbell, who falls face-flat on the floor and doesn't try to stand up again. Tears forming, I shrug. 'I think so.'

'*Ohh*, Anna!' Malini moves closer to me and puts her free hand on mine. Her palm is warm with kindness and it makes me think of my mum. I start to cry harder. One of my tears lands on the floor.

'If you had a friend who was too nice, what would you want her to do about it?' I ask Malini. My nose is running and my voice is shaking but she doesn't look grossed out. She gives me the same calm look that Ben did when I first told him about all of this.

'Well. I'm not sure I'd want her to *do* anything, unless she felt she was being taken advantage of. Is that what you're talking about, Anna? Is this about you?'

'Yes,' I sob. I tell her almost everything, leaving out the part where Marla called Ben my boyfriend and trying desperately to keep the story succinct because god forbid I take up too much of anyone's time. I end with the argument from the other day, bitterness spilling out of me as I talk. 'I tried to assert myself then, to say no and spend the evening how *I* wanted for once, and Marla hated it. She *hated it.* So then we argued and I ended up yelling at her about a load of stuff that she had no idea I was even annoyed about in the first place. And now it's a mess. Just . . . everyone hates that I'm too nice. It bothers them – they always think it's pathetic, or annoying, or whatever, but only when it doesn't benefit them. As soon as it works in their favour, they're all fucking for it.'

I don't realise I've sworn until the word leaves my mouth, but I don't think it matters. Malini is looking at me with so much compassion that I feel even sadder. It makes me want to

Sophie Jo

howl in her lap, defenceless, or run in the opposite direction and kick something.

'I don't understand what I'm supposed to do,' I say quietly. 'Nobody likes me as I am. They want me to be all *ballsy* and outspoken, like Marla, but yesterday Aleks and Natalie were complaining about how difficult she is. So you can't even win.'

'Who's *they*?' asks Malini thoughtfully. 'Who wants you to be ballsy and outspoken?'

I ponder the question. 'I don't know. Everyone. The world.'

'Hm. How do *you* feel about yourself, Anna? I know that Marla's words were what sparked your challenges, but I wonder if a lot of this pressure isn't actually coming directly from other people. It sounds like it might be coming from you.'

Her theory is so excruciatingly accurate that I say nothing. I don't even know how she's come to this conclusion. Nothing I'm telling her makes any sense.

'Sometimes,' she continues, 'when you're a very kind person, it can be easy to wish you weren't. People don't always understand it. Some of them try to take advantage of it.' I nod. 'Do you remember *Gossip Girl*? I used to binge-watch that show when Ben was little, even though I was probably far too old for it, and I always used to tell myself that I should be more like Blair Waldorf. She was one of the main characters, and she was this rude, sassy thing. She always said what she meant, and she didn't care if she offended people. I adored her. I used to wish so badly that I could emulate that in my own life. But realistically, not many of us would want to be friends with Blair. She would make *me* cry on a daily basis. I know that Marla isn't like that, but I do wonder if maybe you've built up Marla in your head as being this very bold, straight-talking person you should aim to imitate. Someone that nobody would ever mess with or find fault with. And my take is . . . that's not true. You've seen first-hand that it's not true.'

'I guess.' I think back to the times Aleks and Natalie have raised their own frustrations with Marla. The way she acts when it comes to Carl – like a sad little girl with everything to lose.

'It's *so* great you're taking steps to grow in this way, Anna,' says Malini, her hand still on mine. 'I wish I'd had the same awareness at your age. But make sure to cut yourself some slack. Kindness, niceness, whatever you want to call it – it's severely lacking in a lot of people. So don't be ashamed of it. You can be proud of who you are.'

She leans back on the cupboard now, looking over to a large noticeboard on the other side of the kitchen as she takes her next sips of tea. There are colourful postcards dotted across it. Sydney Opera House. Some old buildings. A picture of a green, bear-esque creature that must have come from Charlie. I wonder if you always keep the drawings your children do for you, or if you ever take a quick look and think, *that's one for the bin.*

How can you be proud of who you are when you've spent the

last two months trying to change it entirely? There's a silence while I think on it all. It doesn't feel as if I've completely locked nice-girl-Anna away, but I've put so much weight into trying to toughen her up that I'm scared I might have lost her somehow, scattered some parts of her in another direction.

'I don't think I actually know who I am.' The sentence sounds forlorn and ridiculous.

'Not many people do,' Malini replies, unconcerned. 'And the ones who seem sure of it are often the ones who aren't. Take your time, work it out, but don't beat yourself up in the name of change. You can still be Anna. You're just ... learning how to protect her now.'

I walk the long route home from Malini's this evening, finding myself down roads I haven't seen in a while. The cold night air feels cleansing to breathe in and I take big gulps of it with my nose tipped up towards the sky, noticing sharp, speckled stars above me. Sometimes the thought of outer space makes me feel calmer, like there's no point in worrying about tiny human problems when things like planets and galaxies and black holes exist. It's the same when I watch TV programmes about the deepest parts of the sea, the darkest parts we can't even get to, full of mysterious creatures none of us have ever seen. Other times it all makes me feel so anxious I could vomit.

What kind of a person is Anna Campbell? I tilt my neck right back to absorb the blanket of stars and it makes me feel like god, in a bad way. There isn't an answer that springs to mind.

> **Malini 22:17**
> Thanks for watching Charlie tonight. I hope our chat
> helped a bit. Try to remember, no one is sure of
> themselves all the time. M xxxx

I'm not crying any more, but there are old, icy tears still nestled on my eyelashes and my nose is dripping. I wipe it with the back of a sleeve. Then I send Malini a smiley-face and a little heart and I try to remember that no one is sure of themselves all the time, no one, not even someone like Aleks.

It hurts my mind to think about. Like, what kind of a person is Aleks Kowalska? *Activist,* I think. *Funny. Literal. Fair.* Aleks appears in my mind now, with her hair wrapped up in a towel. *Yeah, but not the same person as yesterday,* she shouts to me from an imaginary bathroom. *That was purple, wasn't it. Today is blue – much more appropriate. We all have to try new things and see if they stick.*

What kind of a person is Ben Brennan? *Nerdy. Outspoken. Closed-off.* But I see him back in Dukes, explaining the concept of his inner circle to me with a conflicted look on his face, because he isn't certain either and he knows his way of being only really exists because his world changed three years ago.

When I get home, I find the niceness notebook and my POSCA pens. I start a new page.

I AM GOING TO GET TO KNOW MYSELF.

Twenty-Eight

Anna 14:44

do you want to walk home together later?

Marla 14:46

yes

Marla's standing on the grass by the front of Broadacre at 4 p.m., her head bowed like she's praying. She doesn't sense me approaching and I feel too awkward to offer a 'hi' like normal so I touch her shoulder gently and it makes her jump. 'Sorry,' I say, flinching in return, and she shrugs. We smile at each other then: shy, small smiles as if we're meeting for the first time. It makes me nervous. I wonder if we've lost something we might never be able to get back.

Come on, Anna Campbell.

'Look,' I say, speaking more slowly than usual to make sure I think things through. I can't remember the last time I led a conversation like this. 'I know this has been a bad start to the year for you, Marls. I really hate that. But my point the other day was that we talk about it a *lot*. I've listened when you've told me about Carl and Becky and Isabella and whoever else. And I'm happy to, because I love you, but sometimes I need a break. I need to know that you're friends with me because you *like* me, not because I'm the only one who answers the phone to you.'

She looks crestfallen. 'Do you honestly think that's why I'm friends with you?'

'I don't know. I don't think you ask for this much from other people.'

There's a long pause.

'I was really sad after Friday,' she says eventually, starting to walk and gesturing for me to follow. 'I know I've probably been a lot to deal with lately, but I would always return the favour if you wanted my help or if you told me you were stressed about something. You just never seem to need it. You always act like everything is perfect, so . . . I don't know. It comes across like you can handle it all. I didn't even realise I was bothering you.'

Everything she's just said whirls around in my head, a mini hurricane. *You never seem to need it.* Wrong. *You always act like everything is perfect.* Do I? *I didn't even realise I was bothering you.*

'How could you not realise?' I blurt, my thoughts turning to words. 'When I blanked your calls, did you not think maybe I wanted you to stop phoning me?'

'No, because you didn't give me any warning, Anna! You can't just go from acting like everything's fine and being all *secretly resentful*' – she wiggles around while she says it – 'to ignoring me and expecting I'll mind-read. You hadn't told me any of this. You never tell me any of this. That's not helpful.'

It feels like I stop blinking for about a minute. A semi-healed blister on my right foot has started to throb as we pace, and I try desperately to remember the last time I informed Marla of my unhappiness about something. All that comes to mind are passive attempts: my sulking as we left Niccolo's, my decision to ignore her phone calls, my half-baked mission to make her understand that I was falling behind on my art because of all the Marla-filled evenings. Indirect, vague hinting and hoping.

But what if I'd done it differently? If I'd said, *no, I refuse to miss my Grandad's birthday*, would she have listened? If I'd answered the phone with, *sorry, Marls, I just want some time to myself tonight*, would she have been OK with that? I don't know. Maybe her reaction wasn't ever the point.

'No,' I agree, and I mean it. 'It's not helpful. I've been trying to set boundaries. Stop being so nice. Not just with you – I mean in general. But I have to test stuff out to see if it works, because I haven't done this before, and when you were annoyed about the phone calls it felt like you'd disregarded what I was trying to do.'

'Well, like I said,' snaps Marla. 'You can't disregard something you don't know about. You can't even *regard* it. You can't do anything at all unless you have the information to hand.' She sounds so *her*, so perfectly Marla. It leaves me smiling, just a little.

'I know.'

'But I'm sorry for what I said about Ryan. The "too nice" stuff. At the restaurant. I'm really sorry.'

I look up at her, surprised. I hadn't realised she'd even remembered her accusation at Niccolo's, much less that she'd apologise for it unprompted. Part of me wants to hug her, to say, *don't worry about it* and end that part of the conversation, but something makes me catch myself. 'Thanks. That was a really hard thing to hear in front of everyone.'

Marla looks pained, as though she knew this all along and was sitting on it, wishing it would go away. 'I think I was jealous. Probably makes me sound unhinged, but I was. Everything felt *off* – first of all the Carl stuff, then Ryan. He kept showing up everywhere and interrupting what we were doing, and . . . I don't know.' She makes a breathy noise, a sad little laugh. 'You know what I'm like with my favourites. Gotta claw on to them, haven't I.'

'New friends don't mean you can't have old friends. I'd always love you the most.'

She waves with her hand, fake-modest, like, *stop*. 'It would be a crime if you didn't.'

'Ryan was going through some stuff,' I tell her. 'I think he still is, to be honest. But you were right – I didn't know that at the time. And I didn't think. I just said yes. Same as when I said yes to babysitting, and all the other things. My dad. The concert. Even stuff from years ago. All the extra school activities. Buying lunch for Wynn.'

Marla pulls a face. 'Fucking *Wynn*. I never liked that girl. We should go round to her house like loan sharks and demand your money back, plus an apology as interest.' She reaches over and grabs my little finger as we walk, clutching on to it like a kite string. 'I'm sorry I didn't tell her to back off. Honestly, I thought you'd do it yourself if you were that bothered, but you never did. I should have just stood up for you.'

I waggle the finger around in her grip. 'Thanks, but that's the point of all this. Learning to stand up for *myself* with people like Wynn. You know?'

'I know. Proud of you for trying something new, AC.'

'Really?'

'Yeah. Think of how many people there are on this planet. Billions! Makes sense you can't be nice to all of them.' She carries on, her voice regaining its sarcastic confidence. 'God, I'm actually quite glad this realisation has happened, you know. I've felt like a proper *ghoul* compared to you sometimes. You're really hard to be friends with.'

We stare at each other briefly while I turn her words over in my mind.

'How?' I ask, genuinely bemused. 'What makes me . . . *not* a ghoul?'

Marla wrinkles her nose at me. I haven't seen her do that in weeks and it warms my stomach like soup. 'Everyone likes you,' she says seriously. 'You notice their haircut. You bother to make conversation while you're eating your pasta at lunch. They tell you about the stupid pseudo-clever film they watched at the weekend and you actually give a shit. And then I pop up, like, "Hi! It's me, Anna Campbell's horrible friend! I'm here to point out what's *wrong* with everything."' She sighs. 'Is life easier when you're nice?'

'No. It isn't,' I say, aching with love for her yet still irritated by her question. 'It's just lots of tiny disappointments, one after the other. You get really scared of hurting people's feelings. You cancel on your grandfather's seventy-sixth birthday' – I don't know why I use the word *grandfather*. I hope that it sounds more effective – 'even though he's the only grandparent you have left, because you don't know how to say no. You are always known as the nice one, and if you ever do anything that isn't nice then people lose it, even though *they* do that stuff all the time.'

'So basically,' ponders Marla, one finger in the air, 'we need me and you to merge. And then we would become some sort of perfect human.'

Laughter. Actual shared, authentic laughter.

'Yep. But no one in the world is perfect. Not even us together,' I say, trying to channel Malini in a way that sounds natural.

The Nicest Girl

And then I push it further. 'Not even Carl.'

The gig feels like a dream, or a long time ago. I haven't told Marla what I thought as we walked out – that Carl didn't look happy to be without her, that he didn't appear to really care about Isabella or the attention she was paying to his lap. That when he saw Marla, every single day from the last six months seemed to flash through his face for a second – hurt and hope and anger and something else, some painful disappointment I couldn't read. I don't think it would have helped, and I could have been wrong about it anyway.

'I never said he was perfect,' whispers Marla. She shakes her head gently. 'I just knew he would leave.'

'Have you spoken to him?'

'No. I don't think we will now. Before the concert I kept thinking it would go one way or the other. Like, either he'd be proposing to Isabella in a corner somewhere, or he'd see me and cry and we'd get back together and all of our problems would go away. And it was neither of those things, was it? It was the exact same as it's always been – just . . . somewhere in the middle, take what you want from this, Marla. Trust him or don't. And I don't. But I thought about it, and I don't think it's Carl's fault. I wouldn't trust any of them. *Men*. Not properly.'

She says this in a tone that's deflated and brave at the same time – like she's finally made peace with feeling this way forever. All of it leaves me sad.

There are people you meet who seem to have no business

227

being the way they are. I notice it in them, like when I met my dad's boss, Duncan, who kept saying, *what do you* identify *as, then, Anna? Can be anything these days, apparently*, and doing a horrible booming laugh that sounded like it would have been hard work to produce. My dad had apologised later, *Duncan is a strange one; he thinks a lot of himself*, and I wondered why this was the case. Duncan seemed like the kind of person who should have thought very little of himself and strived for better. But then I'll notice the exact opposite in others – the ones who should see good things but only ever seem to swoop in on the bad, aiming sudden kicks at themselves like it'll help. We all know it's a waste.

As we walk side by side, I feel angry at the waste and what caused it in Marla. I wonder if she and Carl were meant to last longer – maybe not forever, but for a while at least – but it got ruined, picked apart bit by bit because something happened last year that made Marla feel like men are always pretending.

'They won't all be like your dad,' I tell her. The second the words leave my mouth I know that I've crossed a line but I carry on anyway, because why bother if you're not going to be honest. 'They can't be. That's like . . . that's like saying, "everyone you care about will ditch you eventually and move to another city" just because my mum did.'

It's the first time I've mentioned my mum voluntarily for a while. Oddly, it feels less overwhelming than when somebody else talks about her first and expects a response.

'Your mum was honest about it, though,' says Marla, her eyes accusatory. 'She was unhappy, and she told your dad the truth, and it was hard but she did it. She didn't *sneak around* behind his back for months with someone else and then get forgiven anyway.'

It's a fair point. 'I get you. But you can't write off half the planet because of something one person did. What about my grandad?' She looks at me, knowing what's coming, and I continue spouting whatever it is I'm even spouting at this point. 'He adored my grandma. You met them – you saw them together. He would *never* have done anything to hurt her like that. I know it.' I really do. 'And what about Mr Bains?' Marla rolls her eyes now. 'He talks about his wife all the time. Remember that lesson in Year 10 when his laptop background came up on the projector and Hayley was like, "sir, is that Mrs Bains?" and he looked all proud and told us the story of how he proposed?'

'Things are good for a bit, and then they're not,' says Marla flatly. 'Mr Bains isn't that old. He'll probably be bored of her in five years.'

I swallow down the rest of my argument. Instead I say, 'What are you going to do about all this, Marls?' in a voice that sounds more concerned than I wanted it to.

Marla starts to cry. I hold her hand tight, like we're in a film and she's giving birth, and she squeezes back, like she is and it's painful. 'I don't know,' she says. 'I don't know.'

We're at my house now, and, as we sit close to each other on the wall outside the front door, it's as if Marla suddenly becomes aware of herself. She stops sniffing and draws herself up regally. I can feel the love behind it, the new consideration of what I've told her. 'What about you, anyway? What's the latest with babysitting boy?'

I briefly tell her about Ben's trip to Berlin, keeping things short in case he's still a controversial topic.

'Yeah, but when's he back? Because you said he was helping you with things,' says Marla. 'And I want to know – what *are* "things"?' She raises her eyebrows at me suggestively.

I feel the heat across my face instantly. 'Oh my god.'

She crosses her arms. 'It's your fault for not providing me with the details.'

So I provide her with them. I tell her about the niceness notebook – all of the videos and articles – and about Ben finding it. About the challenges, and the woman in Dukes, and Niccolo's, and my dad, and, and, and. An expression I can't quite decipher washes over Marla's face as I'm speaking.

'Well. I wish you'd told me, too.' Her voice is soft.

'I know. I didn't know how to word it. I just wanted to get *on* with the whole thing and skip straight to the end.' Like showing up to a party with your hair curled and your make-up immaculate, pretending you weren't sitting in a damp dressing gown surrounded by discarded skirts two hours ago. 'It's embarrassing.'

'It's more embarrassing that I've been the main topic of all these anti-niceness meetings.' Marla frowns. 'Does Ben think I'm a horrible person?'

Oh. The roles reverse in my head – Marla discussing me, only the negative sides of me, with Carl or some other boy I don't know – and I feel watched. Unfairly judged, like I never got chance to show them the good stuff. 'Of course not. I didn't think of it like that – I'm so sorry, Marls. He knows how much I love you. He's just been encouraging me to stand up for myself a bit more with people. Lots of people. He seemed so *off* when I first met him, but he really isn't. It's strange. He actually cares.'

She tilts her head slightly while I talk, like an interested owl, then springs back into action when I stop. 'I *knew* it.'

'Knew what?'

'Anna Campbell' – she pauses for effect, as she's prone to do – 'likes babysitting boy.'

'*What?*' I make a noise that I hope comes out like I'm scoffing, as though I can't think of anything less accurate. Not because there's anything wrong with Ben, but . . . I don't know why. Marla carries on wide-eyeing me, making it clear she won't drop this regardless of whether I confirm or deny, and the attention makes my face hurt.

Say something, Anna Campbell. Say that he's great, but not in that way. Say that you actually think he'd get on well with Natalie, for some reason. Say that you wish he would just buy some T-shirts that fitted him properly.

'There's nothing to tell. I really don't think there is.' I don't think I'm lying, but it shocks me how quickly my mouth stops working when I go to badmouth Ben's extra-large T-shirts. I try to work out what he is to me, how I might be able to explain the relationship we have to someone who knows very little about it.

'*You* have gone redder than Aleks' summer-hair,' hisses Marla cutely, one tiny finger jabbed in my direction. 'Don't start denying this, AC.'

I don't deny it. I say nothing at all. The last couple of months are looping for me, fuzzy pictures appearing and then losing their focus. Lemon drizzle. Tolkien texts. Wanting *so* much for Charlie's brother to sort out his shoelace and talk to me.

'I looked at his nose in Dukes,' I murmur. 'I know it sounds silly, but I looked at his nose when it was all pink from the cold and . . . I felt something. I just didn't know what I felt.'

Marla shuffles up even closer, so close that our arms are touching. I lop my head down on to her right shoulder and she mirrors it. There's almost a novelty in this, in her being the outer head, the protective layer.

'It's the scariest thing in the world,' she says, holding one of my fingers in her hand again. 'But you told the truth just now. And absolutely nothing terrible happened.'

Twenty-Nine

Maybe life will always involve people asking you to do things you don't want to do.

I'm sat on the dining room table, which my dad used to tell me off for when I was a kid. *It'll break!* Today he seems to be allowing it, even though I'm much older and heavier than the last time he warned me. He's in the kitchen, padding about making coffee and telling me he'll join me in a minute. *I need to talk to you about something, Anna.* I swing my legs, agitated, and the table creaks threateningly.

What could the *something* be? He's got a new job, possibly. Or a girlfriend. Oh my god, I bet he's got a girlfriend. I bet she's been round to the house lots when I've been out and she has a favourite mug – the blue one with the flowers on – and this whole time I didn't even know she existed. *What's her name?* In the space of three seconds, I think of a hundred other scenarios involving my dad and a faceless woman. Dinner dates. Conversations about exes and marriage and children. *Of course – I would never try to replace Gemma*, concerned faceless-girlfriend says, like she's an incoming step-mother from an American movie for kids. I laugh to myself, partly because of the step-mother thing but mainly because I've realised I'm Marla-ing, hard. My dad carries on, oblivious. He shouts from the kitchen to ask if I want a biscuit. I say, 'yeah, go on, then.'

He emerges a few seconds later with a side plate. The plate has four digestives on it, neatly laid out as if I'm a guest at Christmastime, and it's somehow calming and anxiety-inducing at the same time. My dad is not a plate-of-biscuits kind of a man. He lays it down gently on the table behind me and takes a seat on the sofa.

'Anna,' he says, clearing his throat. He looks borderline petrified, so I say nothing and leave him to do what he needs to. *Go for it. Tell me about your girlfriend and her coffee mug of choice.* 'I wanted to talk to you about your mum.'

Abruptly, I stop swinging my legs. Then I become too conscious of the silence. I twist around slightly to pick up one of the digestive biscuits. I break it in half, then put one piece into my mouth and chew. I say, *mm-hmm*.

My dad seems relieved, like this has already gone further than he predicted. He's drumming his fingers nervously, but when he sees me glance at them, he stops. 'She got in touch last week to ask about her birthday in November. She'd really like you to go and stay with her – or just visit for the day, if you'd prefer that. I . . . well, I know it's been a while, hasn't it. But she's hoping this might work for both of you.'

'Why did she ask you? When do you even talk to her?' I demand. The fact that they still speak has surprised me more than I'd be happy to admit.

My dad smiles sadly. 'We do still share a child together, love.' It makes me feel stupid. I pretend I have an itchy nose and think about how often they get in touch with each other. What they discuss. 'She wanted to ask you directly, but I think she's reached out a few times without hearing back. She doesn't blame you for it,' he says hurriedly, putting his hands up to indicate a lack of criticism as I stiffen. 'She understands, but I think this was probably the best option she had.'

The best option she had, I think, *was to stay in Birmingham and not abandon her family.* It's too late now. What's the point? I try to picture us together in London – her showing me Covent Garden, taking me to museums I haven't heard of. Visiting local coffee shops and waving at people I don't recognise. *I didn't know you had a daughter!* Stopping on the sofa in a flat that smells unfamiliar, looking up to see her hairbrush and her glasses and everything else that's supposed to belong in the house with me and my dad.

He asks if I'd consider it. I shrug.

'I'll tell your mum that you'll think about it,' he offers kindly. 'Maybe you could have a chat on the phone first – then it won't feel so strange if you do go to see her?' I do a very small nod, and he treads on, suddenly switching from dad-mode into something rawer. 'Look, I know this is shit. It's shit for me, too. But your mum's life is her own, and she made this decision. We can be hurt by it and still love her.'

It hangs in the air above us.

'You still love her?' I feel embarrassed to use the word in front of him.

He bites at his lip, stalling. 'It doesn't switch off like a tap.'

'Well, it should,' I say, and a few tears tumble out of me. He stays where he is. 'I wish I didn't have to think about it. I wish I didn't have to speak to her ever again.'

'And that's how I would feel, if I hadn't told your mum absolutely everything that I needed to. I cried with her. I got angry. I told her she was selfish, that she'd made a huge mistake. And she listened to me. Now?' His eyes widen. 'Now, I don't feel the same way. I will always believe that she could have stayed here – that we could have made it work. But that was what *I* wanted. If your mum wasn't able to feel happy with me any more, she made the right decision to go. She's forty-nine years old, Anna. She put a lot of people first before she chose this.'

You must have to love someone a lot to say something like that about them. There is a different kind of love in not just pretending everything is fine, that you are fine, but in wrenching the honesty out of you, even if it's repulsive and humiliating and it ultimately gets you nowhere. It reminds me of what Marla shouted at me when we argued – that she didn't want nice. That she wanted real, generous, raging.

'Tell her,' my dad says, reading my thoughts again. I didn't even know he had this ability in him. 'Tell your mum how you feel. She wants to hear it. We both want to hear it.'

If they both want to hear it, I think, *then what do I want to say?* The other three digestive biscuits are still face-up on the side-plate and I take one, holding it in my palm while I wait for the words to come. My dad remains in his seat, the side of the sofa he still always chooses.

'You used to make dinner,' I say quietly.

'What?'

'You used to make dinner for us all when mum was here. Why is it always me now?'

He frowns. 'Is it?'

'Name the last meal we ate that wasn't cooked by me or a local takeaway,' I challenge him, and his eyes grow a little. 'Name the last time you cleaned the bathroom, or bought a birthday card without being reminded, or washed your bedsheets?'

'Oh, love. My bedsheets are vile, aren't they.'

I smile at him. 'Truly disgusting.'

'We make it work, though, don't we?' His face has pinkened and he sounds concerned, like this whole time he thought the set-up we'd created was just right for everyone involved. 'I mean, bedsheets aside. Don't you think we do?'

I guess this is where a balance kicks in. Old-Anna might have lied, or said nothing. Just nodded and escaped, ready to silently dwell on this conversation for weeks to come. She might have imagined screaming something too hurtful and explosive, wanting to know why her father wasn't capable of performing the basic life skills other adults seemed to get along with just fine. *If I wasn't here, if I left like she did, would you even remember to eat? Would you use the same towel for a decade? Would you just shrivel up and die?*

The anger's still there, but it's different now. Letting some of it out means that the sharpness goes away.

'Yes,' I tell him. 'We make it work. But a lot of the work comes from me, and . . . I don't think it should be like that.'

'You mean Grandad's birthday present? He loved it, Anna. I told him it came from you. We were just sad not to have you there with all of us – that was what your Grandad *really* wanted. I did, too – we're a team now, aren't we? It wasn't as fun to walk in there on my own.'

'I know,' I say softly, touched by his honesty but mindful not to forget my own. 'And I wish I'd been there. I'm getting better at balancing things out now. But I wasn't just talking about Grandad's gift – I meant the other stuff, too. Around the house. I try to make things easier for you, but it's tiring and it makes me feel like I'm Mu— you know.' I'm not sure if he knows or not, but I don't say any more. *It makes me feel like I've taken on all of the things that she used to handle. All of the things that made her want to leave.*

My dad nods, like he gets it. 'Your mum really kept me in

check. It isn't fair to expect you to do the same.' Then a pause. 'I suppose it isn't fair to expect anyone to do the same.'

The dust on the coffee table glistens in the afternoon sunlight and my dad glances at the empty space next to him, then up to me. I offer him the plate of digestives. I wish that we'd done this months ago.

Anna 18:08

hi mum. if you want to do something for your birthday then i'll be there

Anna 18:10

i didn't understand before, but i think i do now.
you got better at putting yourself first x

It's 6:10 p.m., which means my mum will have finished work for the day. She'll be sitting somewhere in London with a cup of her favourite peppermint tea, probably listening to the same radio station as always, probably wearing the same clothes she wore when she lived here, in this house. But she's changed now, because she chose to. Because she worked out the same thing that I did: you can't always be the perfect girl who doesn't mind.

Thirty

The dog I drew a few days ago – a tiny poodle lying next to a cactus – is now pinned up on the noticeboard in Malini's kitchen. *Charlie's named him Parker*, Malini told me earlier this evening, and I scribble it underneath the illustration with a pink crayon. Parker sits proudly between a beach postcard and what looks like an old shopping list. Eggs. Blackcurrant squash. Noodles.

There's a loud hiss outside – a firework, early for Bonfire Night and the first I've heard this year. I move over to the window and part the blinds, peering out into the night like a child. Another one goes up and this time it's a bang, followed by tiny golden crackles. Then green. Red. My feet are warm and my breathing is slower.

Anna 20:32
fireworks!! look outside

Anna 20:32

i'm at malini's so you should be able to see them ☺

Marla 20:34

omg i can!!! what a dream

Marla 20:34

we should go see an actual display again

Marla 20:34

if u want

Anna 20:34

yes i do want

Marla 20:38

♥

I carry on watching the fireworks for a while, waiting around during the interludes and cheering internally each time things start up again. The dark kitchen feels calm and cosy, and I stay still, even after one particularly long break that I'm pretty sure signals *The End*. I watch as my breath mists up a small patch of window and in that exact moment it's like my mind takes a photo so that this can be something I remember for a long time. Sometimes I can feel it happening in front of me –

unremarkable things frozen for a second, like a different kind of déjà vu. Like my brain says, *yes, I'll keep this one. I won't forget it, not even when you are eighty, or dead.*

It must be because I like it here. I like the safety of this kitchen, and I like Malini, and Charlie, and the noticeboard with Parker on it, and *god*, I think I like Ben, too.

He must have come in quietly tonight, because I hear his voice before I see him. 'Hello,' he says from the kitchen doorway. His tone sounds different to normal. Surprised.

I pull my head out from the blinds. 'Ben!'

He's still got his hood up and his nose is tinged with pink from the cold again. He grins as he walks over to me, and for a moment I'm sure that we're going to hug, but we don't. I think I imagined it. We just stop a few feet from each other.

I rush to talk. 'How was Berlin?'

'So good. We did the Reichstag, and the Holocaust Memorial, which was . . . well, I guess it feels odd to say it was *good*, actually, but . . . I don't think I'd ever have the right word for it. Do you know what I mean?'

I know what he means. He tells me about other things, too – the pizza they ate, a funny story involving Amrit in the hotel room, the 22,375 steps he did on Thursday – and then suddenly he looks at me like he's just thought of something great. 'It's freezing outside. Can I interest you in a world-famous Brennan hot chocolate?'

'I don't know. What makes a Brennan hot chocolate different

from any other family's?' I ask, teasing.

'We use Charlie's vomit in it,' he says, deadpan once more. 'No. *No!* It's just a powder, truthfully, but we have whipped cream and we have mini marshmallows, and I think you'll find most families save that shit for Starbucks. Right?'

I laugh, caught off-guard, the kind of laughter that I know makes my face look like the photos of me howling as a kid. Dorky, authentic, with the date stamp in the corner. Ben waggles a mug at me as if to say, *cheers*, and sets to making the drinks. I pull myself on to the counter-top and watch him.

'You didn't tell me what happened with you and Marla, by the way,' he says, pausing for a second to roll up the sleeves of his hoodie. 'I know you argued, and I know you made up, but I don't know any of the in-between. Is she OK? Are *you* OK?'

I tell him about the conversations with Marla, making sure to include all of the detail. 'It feels like I'm actually getting somewhere. I've never been that honest with Marla before – it was like I didn't think she could handle it, or something. Or *I* couldn't handle it. But we could. We did.'

He hands me a hot chocolate, complete with sauce drizzled on top of the squirted cream. '*Yes*. That's like challenge number one hundred. The final boss of challenges. Are you proud? *I'm* proud.'

I swell up. 'I guess I am, yeah.'

'Does this mean you're done with the niceness stuff? Or are you planning to keep going? I mean, like, after that . . . what's next?'

What's next, Anna Campbell? Suddenly I'm shivery, standing on the highest diving board with a queue forming behind me. It's daunting but if you wait for too long, it gets worse. If you wait for too long, you'll just have to climb back down the ladder and go home.

'I like you,' I say. No padding. No apology. No Campbell Ramble.

'Oh,' says Ben, and I'm relieved he doesn't ask me to explain myself. He seems to understand what I mean as soon as I say it.

He doesn't say it back.

'I only just realised, I promise.' There's so much air in my chest right now. It sits heavy, like a boulder. 'It's not a Ryan thing – I don't want you to think I've been feeling this way the whole time and lying to you, because I really haven't. It crept up on me. It made me jump.'

'Huh. Well, it's the first time my world-famous Brennan hot chocolate has had an impact like this . . . ' he says, and he's joking but I can still feel a panic radiating from him, this whole thing swamping his thoughts.

I do a half-laugh, half-sigh, picturing dust settling around us. It's done now, and I can't take it back. What did I expect? That he'd have had the exact same epiphany as me, at the exact same time as me, and come back from Berlin ready to share it? Did I think he'd take my hand and say, *Anna, thank goodness, because I've liked you all along*? It'd be awful if he'd liked me all along – if he'd just been helping me to see what he might get in return. It'd ruin everything.

There's a silence while Ben moves over to the kitchen table and sits. He's carrying his mug in one hand and he places it down in front of him, taking hold of it with the other hand too, almost protective. I follow him and sit on the other side of the table, moving a stuffed elephant from the chair. After a few seconds I pick the elephant back up and put it on to my lap. Then I talk, brave again.

'I feel like ... I feel like *me* with you.' I swallow, unsure of how to explain this. 'Normally I'm panicking, always trying to work out which parts of myself to bring out or hide away. And when I'm with you ... I don't need to do that. It doesn't feel strange to cry or shout or laugh or tell the truth. It just feels normal.' A rogue firework fizzes outside, late to the party. 'When I'm with you, being myself feels normal. That's what I wanted to say.'

Ben looks up from his hot chocolate. Smiles, in the way that he smiles. 'Wow. That's the nicest thing I've heard in a while.'

Nice? I freeze, not sure if he's mocking me, and my voice wobbles. 'What?'

'You feel like yourself with me?'

My stomach relaxes. 'I do.'

'Maybe 'nice' was the wrong choice of word. But it *is* nice. I'm sorry, Anna Campbell, but sometimes things are just nice, they're *so* nice, and people have to deal with it.' His eyes sparkle, and I clutch the elephant tightly in my arms. 'In the spirit of telling the truth: this isn't anything I'd thought of before. We've been friends. We agreed we were friends. And I like friends. The inner circle ones, anyway. I like Tuesday evenings. You're *the* most interesting, Anna.'

I beam at him, touched. 'So are you.' I'm swimming in the water now, squinting back up at the boy behind me on the board, willing him to dive in too. I don't know what's in his head – if he's scared, or excited, if he didn't even want to climb this ladder at all – but I think he should jump. I want him to follow. 'I like friends, as well. I like Tuesday evenings. Nothing has to change if you don't want it to. But if it did . . . I think we'd like that, too.'

He nods at me, his face serious. 'You know I normally trust your opinion on things.'

I return his nod, sincere, and it feels like maybe there's something here now, maybe a comma where there could have been a full stop.

We sit silently for a moment, digging for sodden marshmallows at the bottom of the mugs in front of us. My brain takes another photograph.

Thirty-One

Carl's birthday was the day before Halloween, and I never heard about it.

It's only as I sit in the common room on Wednesday, squished happily in the middle sofa spot between Aleks and Marla, that this dawns on me, and for a minute I don't believe my own discovery. It was Halloween on Saturday and Marla and I spent it together in her yellow bedroom. Neither of us did costumes this year. *I really can't be bothered*, I said, voicing a thought I would have kept wedged away last year, and Marla, to my surprise, agreed. Instead, we lit candles and made tofu stir-fry and watched *Scream*, which in our shared opinion is the greatest Halloween film of all, even though the element of surprise has long gone. When she went downstairs to top up our drinks, I sat there content for a few minutes, sniffing sweet pumpkin scent and feeling the weight of the duvet over my legs. I looked up at the printed photos on that one wall, the Marla-and-Anna montage I like to nose through when I go round. It didn't make me feel nostalgic for some other time any more. Just happy.

And the whole evening, Marla mentioned nothing about Carl. I know it was his birthday on the thirtieth, because she told me – she told me weeks ago and reeled off a list of potential couples' costume ideas for his annual fancy dress party. Kurt and Courtney. Sid and Nancy. Mick and Marianne. Marla would have known the party was on Saturday. She would have felt the fact in her mind all day, shoved it out of sight when she needed to, and managed to make everything about us, instead.

Now, I turn to my right to smile at her. She scrunches her nose up like a sleepy cat, oblivious.

'Marla, Christmas is so far away that I'm genuinely offended you just mentioned it,' says Aleks. Her feet are resting on the table in front of us. 'Next weekend, I could deal with. Any further ahead than that . . . get out.'

'It's *November*,' says Marla, pulling a face. 'What's far away about next month?'

You're wishing your life away, girly, Malini and my mum echo in unison. Marla glances at me, as if she hears them, too.

There isn't ever any downtime with her, not really. Blossom becomes sandcastles, sandcastles turn to horror movies, horror movies make room for fairy lights before the whole process starts anew. With Marla, everything moves one step ahead, all of it is anticipated.

'Life is better when you know what's coming,' she says simply. But she sighs a second afterwards, like she's tired.

I've got an A1 board with me today, one of those black ones that says, *I know what I'm doing*. I don't, of course, not fully, but my work is managing to move from hurried guesswork to something more solid, something I could actually want to show people at the end of term. Bold blues, risky pinks. Vivid, like angry flowers. These things take time, and I make sure I have it.

Ryan's seated in the empty form-room when I walk in to collect my board. Miss James is in the next chair along, her hands resting on her lap, her body swivelled towards him. Ryan jumps when he sees me, startled, and moves to get up.

'Sorry,' I say. I get the feeling I've stomped on something already-delicate. 'I just need to get my art board.' But he's gone.

Miss James winces, then catches herself.

'Will he be OK?' I ask. She looks at me questioningly, trying to work out if there's an extra level to what I'm asking here. 'Everything with his dad, it . . . it sounds awful. We don't really speak any more, but I still care about him. I want to make sure he's not dealing with this on his own.'

I know she won't reply properly, not in the human way I want her to, because it's private and personal and she isn't sure that Ryan's told me anything at all. I know Miss James, and she won't breach his trust like that. But she nods at me, kind and clipped at the same time.

'Broadacre is here to support him. Thanks, Anna.' When she

says that, it's like she picks up a weight from a hidden pocket somewhere on my body and tucks it into hers. *Go. Leave it. This problem is bigger than you, and it isn't yours to solve.*

I take the board and walk away.

'Oh, great job, Anna!' Mrs Gana calls from her desk in the art block. She points at the work under my arm and it feels like I glow, just a little bit. 'These Everyday People are looking better and better. Who's this one?'

I tilt it up to show her. 'It's me.'

'A self-portrait. Wonderful.'

I lay my board down on the table, at the spot where Ryan used to sit. Stuck to the centre is a large mixed-media piece: paints and pastels and collage that somehow manage to make up me. My lips are bright-red magazine words. My long hair swirls around my face like liquid and my eyes are giant layered shapes, a multitude of brushstrokes on the page. I've edited this Anna a thousand times – added bits in, taken parts away, tried things out to see what feels right. And that's OK, because I'm not just a watercolour. Marla's more than an oil painting. I'm not just nice, she's not just blunt.

We're all a lot of things.

Thirty-Two

Ben 23:03

You, Anna Campbell, are invited to a Lord of the Rings movie night at mine (you know the address) this weekend (if you are free, obviously). All three films may be a bridge too far, so I say we start with The Fellowship . . . and see how we go. You bring the snacks, I will provide the Brennan family hot chocolate. Do you accept?

Anna 07:05

yes. yes, i really do

Acknowledgements

I wrote a book, and you just read it! Oh my god. Let us take a second to acknowledge THAT.

Thank you so much to everyone at the Madeleine Milburn Literary Agency – particularly to my agent, Chloe Seager, who has been a constant source of wizard-y knowledge and guidance. It does not feel remotely dramatic to say that the Madeleine Milburn mentorship scheme changed my life, and I will be forever grateful for the opportunity to get to know Avione, Francesca, Nigar, Ronali and Sophia, my fellow mentees. Thanks also to Alice Sutherland-Hawes, of ASH Literary, for your encouragement and kindness at the start of this process.

My editor Emma Roberts – for explaining what an em dash is (Who knew! Sure as hell not me.), for regular Disney-themed chats, and for working your magic on many, many versions of my manuscript. You 'got' Anna from the get-go and your expert help and questioning has made *The Nicest Girl* what it is.

Hazel Holmes, Charlotte Rothwell, Becky Chilcott, and the UCLan team and students, especially Samantha Derosia, Amy Rice, Helen Donald and Megan Whitlock, whose wonderful cover ideas were used for the final book you're holding in your hands. UCLan has been so welcoming and so invested in the themes of *The Nicest Girl* – thank you to you all.

My pals – Emily, Vicky, Brittany, Libby, Rach, Leah, Jord, Charlie, Harper and Rachel. I have been talking about this for the longest time and you have been there throughout the whole thing: analysing covers, asking questions, every bit as excited as me. I am so lucky to have friends as supportive as you.

And to my family and extended family, who care so much about *The Nicest Girl* despite the fact that I am a cagey perfectionist who wouldn't let them read a single word until it was 100% finished. I will always be grateful to my mom for spending a significant chunk of my childhood making sure I knew the power of a good book.

Tom – thank you for listening to endless drafts (even though you are Not Much Of A Reader), for giving me pep talks when I needed them, for providing regular Diet Coke fuel (even though you are Concerned About My Habit) and for reminding me that art is hard but always worth it. I really love you.

Real-life Anna Campbells, I see you. Keep going – you deserve to have your say.

PS. If your family feels a little bit like Ryan's family, Women's Aid can help. Nobody should ever have to feel unsafe or on edge in their own home. Visit **thehideout.org.uk** for more information.

If you liked this, you'll love

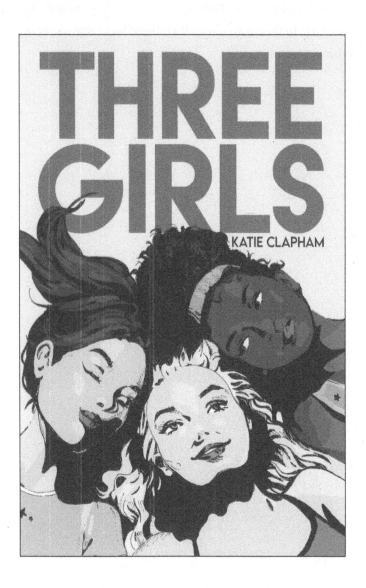

NATASHA DEVON
Toxic
Is she your best friend
or your worst enemy?

BRYONY
PEARCE

Black magic just met
its match ...

RAISING
HELL

EXIT
New York Times
bestselling author
A. J. HARTLEY
IMPERVIOUS

'Delicious and gruesome – will ignite a new generation of vampire fans' LAUREN JAMES

MINA
and the Undead

MYSTERY

Be Kind
Rewind
◄◄

Amy McCaw

YA

VHS

ROSE EDWARDS

This whole
kingdom floats
on a sea of blood

Plough the fields
and it comes
seeping up

The
HARM TREE

"A rich, compelling epic" MELINDA SALISBURY